PRIME ENFORCER

PRIME ENFORCER

VALERIE'S ELITES BOOK 4

JUSTIN SLOAN   P.T. HYLTON   MICHAEL ANDERLE

To Family, Friends and
Those Who Love
To Read.
May We All Enjoy Grace
To Live The Life We Are
Called.

— Michael

LMBPN Publishing
PMB 196, 2540 South Maryland Pkwy
Las Vegas, NV 89109

First US edition, November 2017
Version 1.04, September 2021

CHAPTER ONE

Valerie glared at the man running along the alley—the Pallicon she had told to meet her at the exact spot he was running away from. Dammit, how was she supposed to make any progress when these bastards kept betraying her?

"Didn't I tell him he had one hour to get back to me?" Valerie asked.

"I still say that was generous," Robin replied. She stood next to Valerie on the rooftop under this wide dome of the moon's hybrid space station on the outskirts of the Vurugu planetary system. Her body armor hid her petite but curvy frame, and Valerie was glad—fewer distractions always meant for better mission results.

And at times, the younger woman's body was definitely a distraction.

Their mission was paramount—a journey through a foreign galaxy to find a legendary Lost Fleet, while also hoping to track down an evil shapeshifter and stop him from raising an army to face off against the Etheric Federation. Hell, if that wasn't a challenge worth writing home about, Valerie wasn't sure what was. Lately, though, they had been spending a lot of that time simply flying to reach their destination, which had meant a lot of downtime. It had been a time of getting to know her team better—finding out, for example, that Corporal Flynn enjoyed air drying and wasn't bashful in the slightest, or the fact that Sergeant Garcia snored like three bears trying to kill a fourth with loud snores.

And while she and Robin weren't as close as they had been when they were on Earth, this trip had made her miss the woman more and more. Although she was right next to her, the fact that they didn't touch or kiss made her feel farther away than ever. She missed the days when they'd been back home on Earth, where it had been different between them—at least for a little while.

On that note, she wondered if anyone from home had been writing to her, and if there were a way for a letter to do so.

No matter—at the moment, she was pretty sure Talrok was on this space station, but she wasn't sure how to find him. He'd no doubt taken on a different persona, since he could change his face at will. Maybe finding him would keep her mind focused; allow it to drift to nostalgic moments less often.

"You're letting him get away," Robin reminded Valerie. "He might be the only one who knows if Talrok is actually here, or be able to point him out."

"I'm not letting anyone get away," Valerie replied with a wistful smile. "I'm just making a game out of it. Giving him a head start."

"You…have issues."

Valerie laughed. "Oh, dear—you have no idea."

With that, she nodded at her friend and took off along the rooftops. These weren't the normal sort of buildings from back on Earth; they were more like domes of glass. Some had views, so that when the two went across the roofs, nearly losing their footing more than once, they received several odd looks from the Pallicons inside. They must have been wondering what these strange alien women were doing.

Valerie lost her footing completely and started sliding toward the ground. Her vampire claws emerged to help her hold on but they simply scraped along the glass, so Robin grabbed her by the wrist and swung her to the next roof before following.

"Thanks," Valerie said when her friend landed nearby. They took off again, but were close enough now that they could move to the ground and not worry about losing sight of him.

"Oh, Ernid!" Robin shouted when they were less than twenty paces away. "Looks like we have a problem."

The Pallicon who was running from the duo looked over his shoulder in terror and yelped, then threw himself forward as if sliding to safety. He came to a stop in the middle of a circular area with buildings around it. Several had balconies full of other Pallicons.

Valerie and Robin were on him in a minute, and Robin tossed him into the sky, where he took on the form of a scared child scrambling for something to stop his fall. When he came back down Valerie caught him by the shirt, and he instantly transformed into an image of her to fight back. She backslapped him and pulled him close, eyes glowing red and vampire teeth showing for full effect.

"Where?" Valerie demanded.

"He's... He's..." The Pallicon's eyes rose to one of the ledges nearby, and he cringed. The Pallicons along the balconies backed away from the edges as two on each side stepped forward with large missile launchers on their shoulders.

"Oh, shit," Robin said, eyes wide. Flames erupted from the back of the launchers and the missiles came at them.

Valerie acted fast, tossing the Pallicon aside as hard as she could, since there was no point letting their only informant be killed—even if he wasn't a great one. She figured there were two options, since the missiles were moving almost as quickly as her brain—jump out of the way, or shoot the fuckers out of the sky.

She opted for the former, turning to Robin and grabbing her hands. "Kick with both legs when I say. Ready? NOW!"

The two leaped into the air, brought their feet together, and kicked off each other. With their vampire speed and power, they flew in opposite directions as the missiles exploded where they had been standing a split-second before.

Sure, Valerie landed on her back and skidded across the ground to thunk her head into a nearby wall, but at least she hadn't been blown to chunks. Jumping up, she quickly assessed the situation. The two ledges where the attacks had come from held Pallicons.

Talrok had to be nearby, but why wasn't Aranaught

attacking? Was it a trap? Was she waiting for the right moment to execute the perfect kill?

Maybe, but Valerie wasn't going to wait around to find out. She had to take those Pallicons out. Doors had already opened on the first floor and a wave of them were running out with weapons—blades and guns. Puffs of dirt kicked up as bullets hit the ground.

Valerie didn't want these Pallicons, though. She wanted the ones on the balcony. She was glad to see an advanced sort of dune buggy charging for her, one Pallicon at the wheel and another firing a mounted gun on the back. The one up top was cheering, and a second later his gun went off—but Valerie out of the line of fire, running to the left and then pushing off a building to catch the shooter. She broke his neck, and dropped him off the back.

She let loose a barrage of bullets before the driver realized she was there, then jerked the gun off its mount. The overheated barrel slammed into the him.

She didn't wait to see what the effect was, because they had just reached the position below the ledge. Using the vehicle's momentum she leaped, putting her enhanced strength behind it, and grasped the edge of the balcony. A Pallicon tried to get her with a blade, but hadn't accounted for her speed and strength. She threw herself up and over and kicked out his legs, then grabbed the knife as it arced down. Her momentum brought her around so she could drive it into his neck, and then she was up and leaped for the next. One spun on her with missile launcher ready but froze, realizing what firing that at this close a range would mean for his continued survival.

"Should've sacrificed yourself," Valerie told him, quickly

stepping to his right and taking the weapon as she push-kicked him from the balcony. A glance showed her that Robin had managed to claw her way up to the opposite balcony, which meant the ground below was clear of friendlies.

The Pallicons down there were confused and turned back to the doors to rush up to the balconies, but Valerie had another idea for them. She mule-kicked a female Pallicon behind her to give herself some room, then fired the launcher at the door below.

The missile hit the center of the group and the doorway, and those who weren't hit were caught in the collapse of large stones. Part of her felt badly, but then again, they *had* been trying to kill her. Worse, they were trying to kill Robin.

When she turned to the three who remained on the balcony with her, one turned and ran out through the door while another jumped from the side. This left only the female, who was still kneeling and holding her ribs where the mule-kick had caught her. Since the situation below was taken care of and Valerie saw bodies falling from the opposite balcony where Robin was, she was fairly confident everything was under control.

"Where's Talrok?" she asked the wounded Pallicon.

The Pallicon glared up at her and shifted forms to look exactly like Talrok. "Here I am! Come and eat my face, you piss-ant piece of—"

Valerie used the missile launcher like a baseball bat to slam the Pallicon's legs out from underneath her. When she landed she was in her own form again, not Talrok's.

"I appreciate that you're loyal and trying to protect

him," Valerie told her, jamming the missile launcher into the Pallicon's chest, "but here's the thing... He wouldn't do the same for you."

"You're wrong," a voice said. She half-expected to see Talrok in the doorway when she turned in that direction, but it was Ernid, her source. "Or maybe *he* wouldn't, but *I* would. Let her go, please."

Valerie frowned, caught off-guard by this, but lowered the missile launcher. "You've got something for me now?"

"Don't do it," the female said, but Ernid took a step to her, collapsed to his knees, and took her hand. He didn't address her protestations, but looked up at Valerie. "He has a hideout—a setup a few cities over—and he's heavily armed. He knew it would only be a matter of time."

"The dick knew you'd fail in this little ambush, and yet he still tried it?" Valerie shook her head. "Do your deaths mean nothing to him?"

"Do our deaths mean anything to anyone?" the female asked. "Get it over with." She closed her eyes, waiting, and Ernid stared up at Valerie with pleading eyes.

"I should kill you all in case one of you is really Talrok," Valerie said, "but that's not my style. You aren't bad just because you chose the wrong side, but pull a gun or blade on me again, and I'll show you what a space vampire is capable of."

She let her eyes glow red, then stood. "The name of this place where he'll be?"

"You can't miss it—it's an old dome that was set up by the first colonists." Ernid leaned over to help the female up, but she cringed in pain. "Will she be okay?"

"You can all heal, right?" Valerie asked.

"Only the most advanced of us," he admitted. "And it's more of a shapeshifter thing than healing, but yeah."

"But not her?"

He shook his head. "We're still learning."

"Then get her to a bed. She should get some rest. If you're built anything like us there'll be a broken rib or three, so watch over her. Don't let her move too much or laugh, and she'll be fine."

The female Pallicon stared up at Valerie, baffled that she was leaving them alive and offering medical advice. "Who are you?"

Valerie smiled. "Haven't you heard yet? I'm nobody… just this system's new Justice Enforcer. Some call me 'the Prime Enforcer.'" With that, she smiled and put her helmet on before turning to find Robin.

"You tried it out, huh?" Robin asked through her helmet's comm. She was sitting in the driver's seat of the dune buggy. The former driver was on the ground nearby. He was moving and holding his head so he was still alive, apparently, but he was going to have a killer headache for a couple days at least.

"The Prime Enforcer thing?" Valerie laughed, dropping into the seat beside Robin. "Yeah, and I kinda liked the feel of it. You?"

"No, I'm not going to use a made-up title for myself. Sorry." Robin got the dune buggy out of there and they headed back to the *Grandeur*.

"I'm telling you, it's okay if it's a name someone else gives you," Valerie protested. "On Earth I was Michael's Justice Enforcer, but here it's like a whole other level, so—"

"Give it a rest. Nobody is going to be calling me 'Ms.

Justice' or 'the Queen of Justice,' or whatever stupid name you want to give me."

Valerie laughed and said, "Nobody but me, Captain Justice."

"Ughhhh," Robin replied, gripping the steering wheel hard and doing her best to focus on driving. "I can't wait to find that douchebag. It'll keep you focused on killing bad guys instead of coming up with lame names for me."

"A month of traveling through space, if that was really all it was, gives a lady a lot to think about. Some of that happened to be a cool title for you. Hate it or not, but I think it's perfect."

Robin sighed, but she couldn't hide her smile.

When they reached the *Grandeur* they ditched the dune buggy and quickly climbed inside, ready to be done with this wild goose chase.

CHAPTER TWO

Kalan gazed up at the small hut built into the mountain high above them. "Are we sure about this?"

Jilla nodded. "As sure as we can be."

They were in the heart of Chmara, a city built on the side of a steep mountain. The city was connected by a complicated network of steep ladders, elevators, and boardwalks rather than roads. The rocky terrain made it a near-certainty that anyone who stepped off the walkways would take a quick and violent trip to the bottom.

Like many of the less expensive homes in the city the one they were approaching was set far back from the main boardwalks, which meant a long climb up a ladder to get to the front door.

"I don't like it," Bob complained. "If this guy looks out the window and decides he doesn't want visitors, he could drop a rock on our heads."

"Maybe that's the point," Kalan said. "Works better than a **Keep Out** sign."

The team had been working leads for weeks, trying to

dig up any information that would give them a clue about where to find this so-called Lost Fleet. While Valerie focused on tracking down Talrok, Kalan and Jilla were working their network of connections from their days on SEDE, the prison ship they'd both grown up on. SEDE babies, or "sabies," tended to look out for one another and share information.

Jilla knew a guy who had gotten post-prison work in the largest shipyard in the system, which had led them to a network of pirates who tracked the movements of large ships. That had brought them to the bottom of this mountain. The Skulla male living in the house at the top of this ladder was a former smuggler who had supposedly had dealings with a mysterious fleet from outside the system.

They were here to see if there was any truth behind the rumor.

"Well, better get to climbing," Kalan said with a sigh.

Wearl's voice came from the apparently empty spot to his left. "I'll go after Kalan. That way when I look up I will see a truly inspirational view."

Bob nudged Kalan. "I think she means your ass."

"Yeah, I got it, Bob." With a sigh, Kalan grabbed the ladder with both hands and started climbing.

At the bottom the ladder seemed sturdy enough, but the higher he went, the more it began to sway. The gentle breeze got more severe, and it rocked the ladder. Kalan clutched the thin wood and tried not to think about the thousands of feet of sheer rock below him.

"Hey, I just thought of something," Bob called when they were about halfway up. "Maybe this ladder wasn't built to hold four full-grown adults at once, especially one Kalan's size."

"Shut up, Bob!" the others shouted.

Despite the human's misgivings, all four made it to the top with nothing more than a few worrying groans from the ladder. All the same, Kalan was relieved step onto the boardwalk outside the small house.

A Skulla male was standing there with his arms crossed and his tattooed face wrinkled into a grimace. He offered no greeting as they approached, just looked at the tattoos on Kalan's and Jilla's forearms that marked them as sabies. When he turned his attention to Bob's tattoo-free arms, his grimace deepened.

"Who's he?" he asked.

It was odd hearing such a gruff voice come from such a small creature. Kalan tried to look as nonthreatening as possible, hoping his friendly smile offset the fact that he towered over the Skulla by more than three feet.

"This is Bob," Kalan said. "He's from outside the Vurugu system. Don't worry, he's harmless."

The Skulla grunted noncommittally. "I'd invite you inside, but...well, I don't like having people inside my house. We can talk out here. I'll help you if I can. It's my duty, after all."

"And you carry it out with such joy," Wearl said sarcastically, but thankfully the Skulla man couldn't hear her. Unlike the rest of them, his translation chip hadn't been enhanced to allow him to hear Shimmers' voices.

It was for the best, Kalan thought. Almost everyone got a bit uncomfortable in the presence of Shimmers, but former residents of SEDE much more so. They'd felt the cruelty of Wearl's fellow Shimmers firsthand.

After they'd made their introductions Kalan told the Skulla what they were looking for, and asked what he could tell them about the mysterious fleet.

"Sure, I remember them," he said. "One of the oddest groups I ever dealt with. Trying to remember what they called themselves. The Lapcords? The Lampers? Something like that. They were as tall as Kalan here, but they were wispy things. Looked like a light breeze might blow them over. Their skin was as orange as anything. I did like their leader, though. He was one of those guys who inspired confidence. You knew right away he could handle himself, and you trusted him."

He seemed to warm up to them as he spoke. His arms were still crossed tightly over his chest, but his expression had softened.

"Anyway," he continued, "they came to me looking for a strange collection of items. They wanted enough supplies to keep them fed for over a year, and a bunch of parts for their ships. They didn't want to deal with the local government on the planet they'd settled on, and wisely so—those stingy bastards would have made them pay through the nose."

"Did you get them the supplies?" Kalan asked.

The Skulla looked at him like he was the biggest idiot ever to fly the galaxy. "Of course. I was very good at what I did. That's why I'm able to live the lifestyle you see before you today."

Bob raised an eyebrow. "Yeah. So luxurious."

The Skulla didn't seem to notice his sarcasm.

"Can you tell us where they are?" Jilla asked.

"I can tell you where they were then. I can give you exact location, in fact. Wait here a minute, and I'll embed it for you." He opened the flimsy door and disappeared inside his hut.

Kalan glared at Bob, willing him not to say anything stupid the male might overhear, and thankfully he stayed silent.

The Skulla came out and tossed a chip to Kalan. "There you go. I put the exact location on there, though I must warn you that it didn't seem like they would be keen to get unexpected visitors, if you know what I'm saying. And they have the weapons to make those visitors feel very unwanted."

"Thanks for the information," Kalan replied, "and the tip. By the way, what's a Skulla like you doing living way out here?"

The Skulla grinned. "Let's just say I had some family-related issues back home. Arguing at the dinner table. Disagreements about inheritances. Them hiring assassins to kill me. That sort of thing."

"Sure," Bob said, "that sort of thing."

"Anyway, moving here was the best decision I ever made. No one talks to me. Like, *ever*. I haven't spoken to another living being for eight months before today. It's been heavenly. I was even thinking about moving farther up the mountain. That way any visitors would have to—"

Something slammed against Kalan's chest, knocking him backward. The blow was so unexpected, so out of nowhere, that it took him a moment to understand what had happened. He reeled backward and struggled to keep his balance, but ultimately failed.

He fell on his ass and glided over the edge of the boardwalk, but as he fell into open air he threw a hand out and caught the top rung of the ladder. He held on with all his strength as gravity pulled him downward and the ladder groaned noisily, but it held.

He twisted and got his feet onto a rung, and scurried back up in time to see Jilla slammed backward, again apparently by nothing. He dashed over and caught her before she too tumbled over the edge.

"What the hell?" she shouted.

"My thoughts exactly," he replied.

Then Wearl said, "Hello, sisters."

Kalan's mind reeled. *Shimmers.* They had been attacked by Shimmers.

Another disembodied voice, this one a bit higher-pitched than Wearl's, said, "You are no true sister to us. You have aligned yourself with an enemy of the Shimmer people."

"Who, him?" Bob asked, pointing to the Skulla.

The Shimmer spoke again. "Kalan Grayhewn led a breakout on SEDE and freed one of our most important prisoners. This was an affront to our honor that cannot be ignored. We are taking him back to SEDE, where he will remain for the rest of his days."

"Ha," Jilla said, getting to her feet. "That prisoner he freed is now the leader of the Vurugu System, which means he's your boss. I don't think he'll take kindly to you throwing his rescuer in prison."

Another Shimmer answered her statement. This one

sounded a bit older, and had a gravelly but feminine voice. "Sslake does not need to know about this. Kalan will be in SEDE, so he won't be able to tell him, and the rest of you will be dead."

The Skulla was watching the proceedings with wide eyes. He looked confused, which was to be expected, Kalan supposed. He couldn't hear the Shimmers, so to him it seemed like these people were having half a conversation. "Are you all okay?"

The Shimmer ignored him. "Kalan Grayhewn, you will come with us now. If you fight, you'll die a thousand slow deaths before our—"

Her voice was choked off.

"I've got her by the throat," Wearl shouted. "The other one's standing to the left of the door."

Jilla immediately drew her pistol and squeezed the trigger, blasting the wall of the house.

"Six inches farther left!" Wearl yelled.

Jilla corrected her aim and squeezed off another round, and the Shimmer shouted in pain.

"Got her in the arm," Wearl said. "Shoot her again."

The Pallicon fired, but something slammed her backward.

"You missed, shapeshifter!" the Shimmer shouted as she crashed into her.

"Let me go!" the Shimmer Wearl was choking croaked.

"You just told me you're going to kill us all and capture Kalan," Wearl said, "so I think not. I don't want to die, and he's way too sexy to spend his life in a cell."

Jilla tried to get up, but something hit her in the face and rocked her head back.

Kalan had about had it with these invisible bitches. He ran toward Jilla and leaped at the space above her.

He slammed into the Shimmer with all his weight, and she let out an "Ooof!"

He wrapped his arms around the Shimmer as they hit the ground and locked his hands.

"Unhand—" the Shimmer he was holding groaned, but that was as far as she got. Fists beat against his sides, but he only squeezed harder.

As soon as she spoke, revealing the position of her face, Kalan headbutted her. His forehead connected with the Shimmer's face, and something cracked.

"Ha!" Wearl said. "You broke her nose."

Kalan felt something wiggle against his side, and realized too late that the Shimmer had pulled her hand loose. Her fist connected with his eye, and his head rocked back.

Jilla crouched next to him and pushed her gun forward until it connected with something solid. "Is this her head?"

"Yep," Wearl confirmed.

Jilla pulled the trigger, and the creature in Kalan's arms stopped struggling.

"Just a second," Wearl said. There was a *crack*, follow by the *thump* of something hitting the ground. "Okay, mine's dead too. Broke her neck."

Bob looked around, a bit perplexed. "Is that all of them? I didn't get to kill any."

Wearl chuckled. "Hey Kalan, your shirt is covered with blood."

"What?" He looked down at his chest. His shirt felt wet, but he didn't see anything. "I take it your blood's invisible too?"

"Invisible to *you*."

The Skulla was staring at the hole Jilla had put in his wall. "Will someone tell me what the hell is going on?" he asked through clenched teeth.

"Invisible assassins tried to kill us," Bob said.

"Huh." The Skulla stood and crossed his arms again, his mouth a thin line. He looked like he was trying to decide whether to believe them, and after a moment he continued, "I think it's time for you to leave."

He'd get no disagreement from Kalan.

The team thanked him again, and apologized for putting the hole in his wall. Kalan gave him all the coin he had on him, a substantial amount he suspected would go far beyond covering the damages. He could probably buy a whole new house.

That was one nice thing about running with Valerie's Elite: they weren't short on funds. Sslake had paid them well for their role in freeing him and returning him to power.

As they descended the ladder Jilla asked Kalan, "You okay?"

"Aside from a black eye, I'm great. You?"

"I'm fine. I meant are you okay *mentally*. You just found out you've been declared an enemy of the Shimmer race."

"So?" he asked.

Jilla paused as if she couldn't believe what she was hearing. "You know what that means, right? The Shimmers won't stop. They'll keep hunting you. Chase you across the galaxy if they have to, and eventually they *will* get you."

"She's right," Wearl, who was below him, said. "We are a persistent race."

"Wonderful," Kalan muttered. "Hey, why aren't they mad at Bob? He was involved in the breakout too."

"Don't bring me into this!" Bob said. "I'm just here to fight for justice and stuff."

"Bob didn't grow up under their care," Wearl explained. "You represent something they deeply fear. Think about how many sabies there are in the galaxy, and imagine if they all got together and used what they knew to take the Shimmers down. You didn't merely insult their honor, you also threatened their business. They can't afford to let you run free. They have to make an example of you."

Kalan reached the bottom of the ladder and stepped off, glad to once again be on semi-solid ground. "You know what? I'm not going to let it distract me. We'll deal with the Shimmers later."

"Kalan," Wearl said, "the fact that they found us means they know you're in this part of the system. And if those two were following procedure, they contacted their commanding officer to say they'd found you before they attacked. The full might of the Shimmers' force will probably be on the way here soon."

"Then let's make sure we're not here when they arrive. We got the information; that's what matters. Now, somebody contact the *Grandeur* to let them know we need a ride." He paused for a moment. "And tell them I need a clean shirt."

CHAPTER THREE

The *Grandeur* landed at the edge of the city where Kalan had said they'd be waiting, and Valerie was glad to be back with the rest of the team. They split up all too often, and while she realized the necessity of it and had been used to attacking on multiple fronts even back on Earth, her preference was to have everyone together.

She liked to see them; to know they were safe, and to know they had her back. Her days of being a lone wolf were long behind her. Now it was about the team, and about friendship.

So it was that when Kalan approached with a smile and friendly wave, she leaped down the stairs to wrap the gray giant in a hug.

"You two almost die or something?" he asked, setting her down.

She laughed. "Can't a gal be excited to see her pals?"

"Ah, I'm glad to see you all too." He held up a small chip. "But I think you'll be even happier when I tell you what's on this chip."

"Tell me it's guacamole and I'll kiss you right now," Robin said, walking up behind Valerie and standing beside here with one arm at her side and her other hand on her hip in a playful way.

Kalan shook his head. "Why would I want guaca-what-ever? Now I'm not so sure I want to tell you."

"Hmm... I have information you might want to hear," Valerie replied with a wink.

"Ah." Kalan turned to Jilla and said, "Think we should trade, then?"

Jilla smiled. "First of all, I think you both are ridiculous. Second, yes! Get it over with already."

"Me first," Valerie blurted. "We know where Talrok is, or where he supposedly is, at least. You have your extra-large Grayhewn boot on so you can shove it up his ass?"

Kalan frowned. "I *think* you're messing with me, but I'm not totally familiar with your Earth sayings yet. Suffice it to say, I don't plan on getting any of his shit on my boot, and would prefer to keep my foot away from his ass in general."

She *was* messing with him, in that she loved to use phrases that would confuse him. His responses always made her smile, and this time wasn't any different.

"Earth-Speak 101, Lesson Five-Hundred and Ninety-two," Valerie said as if she had actually been keeping track. "Putting your boot up someone's ass actually just means bringing a beat-down, as in kicking their ass. It's an exag-geration, though this one time—"

"Val," Robin interrupted, "please don't make up a story about actually losing a boot up someone's ass."

"A stiletto, actually," Valerie replied.

"See, Kalan, that's how you know she's lying." Robin gave her a grin. "This woman wouldn't be caught dead in stilettos, or any sort of heel for that matter. She's all about the Pumas."

"And now these military armor boots," Valerie said with a laugh. "Caught me! Now seriously, can we get to kicking some Pallicon butt? No offense, Jilla."

"Don't kick mine, and we're good," the Pallicon replied.

Kalan was frowning. "I have yet to grasp Earth humor, but will keep trying. In the meantime, I believe it was my turn."

"Ah, yes!" Valerie leaned in, excitedly. "What've you got for us?"

Now it was his turn to grin. "Only the location of the Lost Fleet."

"The hell you do!" Robin said excitedly, stepping forward. "How'd you get that?"

"We Grayhewns have our ways," he replied smugly.

"Of course, he's only alive because of me," Wearl said.

"Thanks again, Wearl," Kalan said. He glanced around, since he was unsure where his invisible buddy was standing.

"We'll go take down Talrok and stop the AI, then go find this Lost Fleet and convince them to take up its old stance on justice and keeping the nearby systems in check." Valerie nodded, liking the sound of that. "Another day in the life of the Prime Enforcer."

"The what?" Kalan asked, confused, then smiled. "Oh, you mean that title you were working up on the way over here?" He turned to Robin. "What was it, 'the Justice Helper?'"

"That was the worst of the bunch," Robin replied with a frown, "and thank you so much for remembering."

Kalan chuckled. "Hey, I'll stop as long as you two don't try to give me some weird nickname."

"Well the Prime Enforcer thing is gonna stick," Valerie stated, then nodded toward the ship. "Got that boot ready for an ass-kicking?"

"I do indeed," Kalan said, leading the way toward up the ramp so they could get a move on. At the hatch he paused and added, "To be clear, my boot is staying on my foot, not coming off inside his ass."

"Perfectly clear," Valerie replied with the straightest face she could muster.

"You're mean," Robin told her after the others were inside.

"You think so? I see it as genuinely helping him learn our ways of saying things. I guarantee he'll remember this one."

Robin nodded, not able to argue that. "I want to know what ways you're messing with me that I don't know about yet," she added as they boarded.

"Oh, I haven't decided how to mess with you yet, but it'll be good when I do."

"Now I've got high expectations!" Robin exclaimed, laughing. "And on that note, why are we so giddy when we're about to go into a fight?"

"It's what we do best," Valerie said, pressing the button to close the door behind them. "Makes sense, right? Others are happy sit back and relax. We're not in our zone unless we're stopping bad guys and gals."

"Someday I hope that won't be true." Robin put her

weapons on the rack and took a seat. "I want to wake up one of these days and have no more enemies out there. Nothing left to worry about, just be able to relax and enjoy myself."

"Sounds boring."

"I'm with Robin on this one," Kalan told her. "You, Bob? Why are you so quiet?"

Bob looked up, hand on his stomach, and grimaced. "Shit, I'm hungry and am sick of smelling the stuff these locals eat. Fighting? Peace? I want a steak, some potatoes, and a glass of beer."

Valerie and Robin broke into laughter, completely understanding. All the foods they were craving popped into their minds.

"Basil on anything," Valerie said. "Or some of my friend's homemade croissants. Oh, they're to die for."

"Sandra's, with the chocolate?" Robin licked her lips and closed her eyes.

"Ah, what about a good bowl of popcorn?" Bob added. "Maybe some—"

"None of us have any idea what you are talking about," Jilla cut in. "Just so you know."

"Well, if you ever make it to Earth, we'll be sure to treat you to the best steaks and popcorn and whatever else we can scrounge up." Valerie leaned back, nodded to Flynn to get them off the ground, and added, "That's a promise."

"One I look forward to you keeping," Kalan said.

Valerie had already told Flynn where to go, so he piloted the *Grandeur* up and the two groups started comparing stories about what they'd been up to in their recent hunts.

"You killed two of 'em?" Flynn asked when Kalan finished telling them about the invisible blood.

"And the more important part of that story," Garcia noted, "was that there are more coming. We need to deal with Talrok and leave ASAP."

"Exactly our thought," Jilla agreed.

After Valerie had related her side of the adventure, she paused to listen to Robin tell them how she had actually been worried for a minute—which was news. The others just nodded and said that sounded about right.

"What has been bothering me, though," Bob remarked. He'd brought some snacks over to the group and talking with his mouth full. "Is Aranaught's absence."

"Not that it's a bad thing," Kalan added, "but it's suspicious."

"Unless they were trying to get us to let our guard down," Valerie said. "Then they hit us hard at the dome. That's why I want us all to be ready for anything that might come our way."

Arlay, who had been on ship's watch with Garcia and Flynn, emerged from the back room and ran a slender hand across her blue head as if combing the hair she didn't have. None of her race did, so the gesture made Valerie curious.

"I've been thinking about that," she said, having apparently heard what they were saying from the other room. "It might be the case, but if Aranaught is really after the Lost Fleet to amp up her power, I'd be willing to bet that's what she's doing. She's not lingering around here trying to trap us, not when she could be amassing a power against which we wouldn't stand a chance."

"But can't she be everywhere at once, in a sense?" Flynn asked. "I mean, as an AI, can't Aranaught be in all places at once?"

"I don't think so," Valerie interjected. "She was based out of that space station. Yes, she had a long reach, but—"

"She gets weaker the farther the signal is from the hub," Arlay finished, nodding and smiling. "At least, that'd be my guess."

Flynn was nodding along and Valerie figured it was as likely to be true as not, so she might as well assume these two knew what they were talking about. Since she hadn't had much exposure to technology like this back on post-WWDE Earth, it was all a bit over her head.

"Well, be ready just in case, and be happy if she's not there," Valerie said, then motioned at the viewport. "Speaking of which, we're not far off now."

Sure enough, they were approaching the dome, its gray-blue glass reflecting in the waning light. Local winged creatures took to the sky at their approach. Valerie happened to glance out and see one, and cringed at the sight of its face, which looked almost like a fanged piglet's. The sooner they could save the universe and go home, the better.

"You ever think it's strange," she asked Robin, "that on an alien planet you don't really know which one is the intelligent species?"

"The ones whose speech our chips translate," Robin replied.

"That's actually kind of smart," Valerie told her. She leaned back, pouting.

"What were you going to say, though?" Robin asked.

"Now it sounds dumb, but...I was thinking that we assume the intelligent ones are those who walk on two legs, pretty much. We've never tried to corner those flying pig things and talk to them, or other species on other planets, right? Maybe *they're* the intelligent ones, with built-up civilizations that are well hidden, and we just never come across them because of our biases."

"You know..." Robin turned to face her. "I have no answer for that. I don't see why it couldn't be the case."

"Something to think about, then." Valerie smiled.

The *Grandeur* was almost on top of the dome now, so Flynn pulled her around to take a peek. The inside looked like a reception hall after a wild party, with tables and chairs lying on their sides. Something moved below, darting across their line of sight, but it was hard to tell what it had been.

"I'm bringing her down there," Flynn said, pointing to a mostly flat area nearby.

It looked to be rocks interspersed with patches of grass, and it seemed as good a place as any for landing. After they secured the ship, they headed for the dome. They all wore full body armor, complete with helmets, and each carried a rifle from the ship's armory.

"And you of course considered that your informant was lying?" Bob asked when they were finally standing outside the dome, looking at more broken windows and a missing walled area.

"I did," Valerie replied. "But I don't think so, and I'm pretty good about this stuff."

"Well then, maybe he went out for groceries?"

Robin laughed, but stopped at a glance from Valerie.

"Move out," Valerie ordered, entering the dome with the others close behind her. They were on the main floor, and there was a curving walkway that led upward. She glanced back and pointed at Kalan and his team. "You're with me. I want to switch it up a bit."

They had left Flynn with the ship, which meant Robin would go through the main floor with Garcia and Arlay.

Something moved in the distance, and they heard a clatter and something banging on metal. Valerie tensed and gestured her team forward. They proceeded up the walkway while Robin and her team moved in the same direction below.

At the first turn Valerie paused, then had an idea. "Wearl, would you scout ahead?"

"I'm on it," Wearl replied.

"Great. Keep moving...and if anything is up there, let us know. Stay in my ear. Got it?"

"Roger that," Wearl said, and the teams went through the building.

"Nothing yet?" Valerie asked.

"Nothing."

They moved on, coming to a floor that had a view of the jungle outside. It was furnished with a long table and racks of what looked to be computer servers.

They heard more crashing ahead.

Valerie turned to Kalan.

"She says it's...a dinosaur?" He frowned. "That doesn't — Oh, shit, get down! She said to get out of sight."

The team dove behind the tables, and a moment later a robotic dinosaur ran past their location. It hit a window and stumbled back, then hit the window again and tumbled out as the window broke.

"There're more," Kalan said, listening, "but they're not functional."

"What the hell?" Bob asked, glancing around.

Valerie's curiosity had been spiked as well, so she ran forward to find the room Wearl was talking about. Sure enough, it was full of half-built robot dinosaurs. Some were complete but had been smashed, as if someone had taken a hammer to them. They were mostly about human-size, with large claws and sharp teeth. Some even had fake skin.

"Someone was trying to create an army of robot dinosaurs?" Bob asked. "Fucking cool!"

"Wouldn't have been so cool if they had been used against us," Valerie countered. "Those claws would've stung worse than a bee."

"We would've used them, had you arrived sooner," an unexpected voice told them, and they heard were gunshots downstairs. Robin's team was under attack.

Valerie had started to head back downstairs when she saw the source of the voice. The wall was in fact a brightly-lit window, through which Talrok was glaring at them.

"Aranaught had gotten them functional and was ready to send them at you, but she wouldn't wait. She just had to be the first to find the Lost Fleet. Just had to do it her way." Talrok stepped closer to the window. "So she abandoned me, leaving me with…this."

More shooting, a scream, and then a *thud*.

"It's over," Valerie said, stepping up to the window. She

could probably reach through and grab him by the throat. "You've lost."

"But it was never truly about me, was it?" Talrok countered. "As long as all of you go down suffering—which you will—I'll be happy. I'll also be a martyr for the cause, if I must. Or..." he reached up, "maybe I'll simply destroy you right here."

He pressed his finger to the window as if it were a HUD, and the view faded. It was a wall again.

"That doesn't strike me as a good sign," Bob said.

"Get the doors," Kalan said, but a slab of metal was already sliding across. It stopped halfway, however. "Thanks, Wearl. Everyone out!"

Valerie was still focused on the wall, and where she had last seen Talrok. She pulled back her arm, bent it, and shouted as she brought it forward, striking the wall with her elbow. After a *clang* and a blast, she flew across the room and hit the opposite wall. Jilla went to her a second later, while Kalan shouted something about cutting him off and he ran from the room.

Valerie heard more gunshots over the ringing in her ears, and then there was another sound: a roar that carried through the hallways.

"Something tells me not all the dinosaurs were destroyed," Jilla said nervously.

Valerie shook her head, clearing it as she stood and recovered her rifle. "That son of a bitch is gonna pay for that."

Being careful not to run over Wearl, who was apparently still holding open the door, Valerie darted out, rifle at the ready. Kalan and Bob were banging against a closed door.

"Valerie!" Robin's voice shouted through the earpiece. "It might seem like we need you here, but don't come down!"

"Why?"

"T-Rex!"

Valerie would've thought in any other circumstance that she had misheard, except that she had just left a room full of robot dinosaurs. Since Earth was in bad shape and had nearly faced total destruction, the extinction of the dinosaurs was something she had spent quite a lot of time learning about. She was still pretty sure their existence hadn't been curtailed by nuclear weapons as humanity's nearly had, but she wasn't completely ruling it out.

When she heard the word 'T-Rex,' she had a vague idea what it meant.

"Do not let him get away!" Valerie shouted, pointing at the door. As she ran she said into her comm, "Flynn, get the *Grandeur* ready. If anyone leaves the dome before you hear from us, shoot to motherfucking kill!"

"Roger that, boss!" Flynn replied. "You need my help?"

"Actually, we might. Stand by."

She followed Robin's instructions and worked her way inward until she reached a balcony overlooking the interior—where she came face-to-face with a two-story-tall robot in the shape of a T-Rex.

Holy hell.

Her first instinct was to blast the shit out of it so she started unloading like crazy, but Robin shouted something about the bullets not penetrating its metal armor. She pulled back as it turned on her, revealing turrets on each shoulder, then dove back through the doorway as rounds started pelting the walls. She kicked the door shut and rolled into a ball as the shots clanged against the door, and then the door went flying off, torn to shreds.

That gave her an idea.

She stuck out her rifle and fired again, shouting, "How's this for a steak?" She kept yelling as she ran, hoping the T-Rex would follow. "Nobody fire on it," she ordered. "Not yet. Flynn, get in the air *NOW!*"

"What're you doing?" Robin asked. "This isn't the time for heroics!"

"Pretty sure that couldn't be farther from the truth," Valerie called, then kicked open another door. She was glad to see a conference room with a full window, from which she unleashed on the T-Rex again.

"Get away from that door," she shouted to Bob and Kalan, and they ran when the T-Rex opened fire on their location. His shots hit the door they'd been pounding on, though, blowing if off its hinges—to the curses of Talrok, who was within.

"What the hell is that?" Flynn shouted over the comm.

"*Now*, Flynn! Open fire now!" Valerie yelled. "Everyone else, get out of here!"

"You're coming, right?" Robin asked.

"Of course—as soon as I take care of our little friend."

The rest ran as Valerie had demanded, and then the turrets from the *Grandeur* opened up on the T-Rex. One glance back showed it was working—that metal armor couldn't hold up to her baby.

When Valerie turned Talrok was holding an alien rifle,

its tip glowing purple. She smiled and shook her head, then moved at vampire speed. Two shots to the head, five to the chest, just in case.

"The target's down," she said, joining the others in their escape. She was with them before they reached the first floor, where Robin and the other two knelt, ready to provide cover fire if needed.

"That everyone?" Garcia asked.

Valerie nodded.

"Flynn, we're out," Garcia said. "Send a missile down that extinct motherfucker's throat."

"Now we're talking!" Flynn came back, adding a "Woohoo!"

"Go go *go*!" Garcia shouted, leading the retreat. After they had made it out—Valerie last, making sure the others were ahead of her—the missile hit the robot and the T-Rex fell backward before exploding into shreds.

The concussion threw her forward and she hit the ground, but quickly recovered.

"Wearl? Wearl!" Kalan shouted, searching for his invisible companion. A moment later his face melted with relief, and he straightened. "She's safe."

"What'ya say you all get on this ship and we go find ourselves a new planet to blow up?" Flynn asked.

"I like the first part of the plan," Valerie countered, waving him down, "but let's not get trigger-happy just because we let you blow up one dinosaur today."

Flynn lowered the ship and opened the ramp, walking back to it to help them up, if needed.

"Anyone hurt?" he asked, giving them a onceover.

There was a blood welling from a gash on Garcia's

shoulder and Robin had been hit in the side, but both would heal fast enough. Flynn wasn't worried about the grunts of pain.

"Too bad it wasn't a real dinosaur," Bob said when they were finally seated and preparing to take off. "We could've had that steak."

Everyone laughed, and Kalan nodded to Valerie. "Quick thinking back there, getting the dino to take down the door."

"Thanks, Kal. Can I call you Kal?"

He frowned. "That sounds like a girl's name, so…no."

"He's right," Jilla chimed in, and Robin nodded.

Valerie smiled and shrugged. "Just trying things out, guys, just trying things out."

A display showed the planet below them growing smaller and smaller as they flew away, and once they were in space Valerie gave them the signal they could relax. They would be able to sleep, clean up, and eat. Before too long they would be at planet Rewot in the Parscal System, so it was better to get all that in while they could.

For her part she was looking forward to each equally, but when she stood up to go get clean she felt a wave of mental exhaustion wash over her. Her eyelids were heavy too, so she leaned back and let nature take its course. Even badass vampires in space had to sleep from time to time.

CHAPTER FOUR

Kalan had spent much of the journey to Rewot—the planet where the Lost Fleet was supposedly hidden—arm-deep in the ship's digital library searching for information on the planet.

During the month it had taken to travel here from Tol's moon, Kalan had spent a lot of time in the digital library. The information he located was fascinating. He learned about the Etheric Federation, about Earth—the planet Valerie and her crew were from—and about alien races he'd never heard of. At first it had been a way to stave off boredom, but then he'd thought that maybe the knowledge would help him in his search for the Bandians—his people.

Eventually he admitted to himself that he kept coming back to it because it was fun. He found he enjoyed reading about all these far-off planets and peoples. The data sparked his imagination, letting him experience a thousand different lives while sitting in his comfortable chair.

Unfortunately, the library did not have much information on Rewot. The planet was categorized as capable of sustaining life, but it was unknown if anything lived there. The climate was simply marked as "volatile," and there was no more information beyond that.

After he'd read through the brief description a few times he got up and made his way to the bridge, where he knew everyone else would be gathered.

"There he is," Valerie said when she saw him. "Our gray antisocial rock-man."

Kalan chuckled. Over the course of this journey he'd gotten to know Valerie and Robin and the others much better. Valerie and Robin had shared a little bit of their past on Earth with him, and his respect for them and their mission had grown. After all the things they'd been through, it was amazing that they were still in the fight and as hungry for justice as ever.

They'd long ago done their part for the greater good. No one would have blamed them if they'd decided to retire to a quiet life, yet on they fought.

It was inspiring to Kalan. He hoped he could remain as dedicated for half as long.

"I was reading about our destination," he said, sinking into a chair.

"Learn anything interesting?" Robin asked.

"Not really. Turns out there's not much information. It says Rewot can sustain human life, which I'm hoping means we'll be able to breathe."

"It's a bit of a longshot, isn't it?" Garcia asked. "Going to a location embedded on a chip by a stranger who remembered meeting a foreign fleet years ago?"

"It's a longshot," Valerie admitted, "but right now it's the best we've got. How far out are we?"

Flynn checked the monitor. "A little over two hours."

They spent the next hour and a half speaking and laughing together. Valerie and Kalan talked about what they'd say to this Lost Fleet if and when they found them.

When they were half an hour out of Rewot, some blips appeared on the monitor.

"What're those?" Robin asked.

Flynn frowned. "Look like five ships. Small ones."

"What are they doing?" Valerie asked.

Flynn sat up a bit straighter. "Flying straight at us." An alarm on the control panel started beeping. "And firing on us."

Valerie hopped out of her seat and ran over to the screen. "Shit!"

Then was another beep, this one slower and longer. "Looks like they want to talk."

"Put them through."

Flynn punched a button, and a moment later a strange lilting voice came through the speakers.

"Attention: you've entered Rewot airspace. Change course now. Those first shots were warnings, but the next ones won't be."

"They've got to be crazy," Bob muttered. "Going up against the *Grandeur* with five little fighters? We could blow them back into their atmosphere with the push of a button."

"I say we give them a warning shot right in the engine," Wearl added. "Disable them, and let them float around up here for a few days thinking about what they did."

"Shut up, both of you," Valerie said. She pressed a button and spoke into the microphone on the control panel. "We are heading toward Rewot, and we are not able to change course."

There was a long pause. "On what business?"

"No use lying," Kalan told Valerie.

She nodded. "We're looking for a fleet of ships that arrived here maybe five years ago. We have important business with them."

Another pause. "There's nothing like that here. Rewot is uninhabited."

"Then why the hell are you protecting it?" Garcia whispered.

Valerie sighed. "We're not in the mood for games. We're trying to find the Lost Fleet. We have one of their allies with us."

"Yeah?" the fighter pilot asked, the hint of a laugh in his voice. "Who's that?"

"A Bandian," Valerie answered.

There was another pause, this one much longer than before.

"At least they're not shooting at us," Bob said.

After nearly a minute, the pilot spoke again. "Please follow us. We'll escort you to Rewot."

Flynn looked up in surprise. "I don't believe it. For once in our lives, something was easy."

As they were passing through the atmosphere, the pilot's voice came over the radio again. "Are you equipped to handle a water docking?"

Flynn's eyebrows shot up. "A what?"

"A water docking. Can your ship land and float on water?"

Flynn looked at the others. "What the hell kind of a

question is that?"

Valerie leaned down and spoke into the microphone. "We haven't tested it, but we're a big fucking spaceship so I'm going to say no."

"Copy that. When we break through the clouds, you'll see a small island in the center of the ships. It should be big enough for you to land on."

"Should be?" Jilla asked.

"Am I the only one who's confused?" Robin asked.

Moments later they broke through the clouds, and it all became clear.

The deep-blue surface of Rewot stretched below them. It was water all the way to the horizon.

Kalan frowned. "Why'd they bring us down over an ocean?"

Flynn adjusted the settings on a monitor. "I'm scanning for landmasses, and not finding any. A few small blips here and there—islands probably—but nothing large."

Valerie grunted. "Huh…a water planet."

Kalan pointed through the window in front of them. "Look."

The water below them was speckled with large, oddly-shaped objects that reflected the light of the system's sun back at them. It wasn't until they were a bit lower that they could determine what these things were.

"They're spaceships," Jilla said, excitement in her voice. "There must be two dozen of them."

"Not small ones, either," Robin added.

She was right. Each was nearly the size of the *Grandeur*, and a few were larger.

"The Lost Fleet," Valerie whispered.

"Those things are parked right on the water," Flynn pointed out. "I guess that's why they asked if we could float."

In the center of the floating dock was a single swath of land—the island.

Flynn set them down gently on the sand-covered island while Bob ran some diagnostics.

"Looks like the air's breathable," Bob said. "We should be good to go."

Kalan grinned at Valerie. "How's it feel? After more than a month of searching, it seems we found our Lost Fleet."

"Ha!" she said. "Here's hoping. But if there's one thing I learned, it's that things are never as simple as they seem at first glance."

She walked to the nearest airlock and opened the door. When he gazed over her shoulder, Kalan was surprised to see a crowd of a hundred or so beings gathered around the ship, looking up at it in anticipation.

Kalan was momentarily taken aback by their appearance. The Skulla had described them simply as orange, as tall as Kalan, and thin. While all that was technically true, it understated the effect of seeing them. They were more than thin. They were willowy, and their thin limbs almost flowed with their movements.

But their most striking feature was their skin. It was a deep and vibrant orange that almost seemed to glow, and it offset their pale-yellow eyes and tiny black irises.

Kalan lingered in the airlock to take in the scene as Valerie stepped onto the sand. It took him a moment to realize that the thing they were all staring at so intently was him.

"It's true," one of them said. "A Bandian. A real Bandian."

Two of the beings stepped forward, a male and a female who appeared to be a little older than the others.

"Welcome to Rewot," the female said. "From your strange expressions, is it safe to assume you've never met a Lavkin before?"

"That's right," Valerie said.

"Let's change that immediately," she said with a smile. "I'm Mej, and this is my husband Lien. We are the caretakers of this squadron."

"Caretakers?" Kalan asked. "Does that mean you're the leaders?"

The two Lavkins exchanged a glance, then Lien said, "Yes, I suppose you could say that. At least temporarily. Mej's brother Lolack is the true leader, not just of this squadron but of the entire fleet."

"Great," Valerie said. "Where is he?"

"He's not on Rewot at the moment," Mej said quickly.

The others had disembarked from the *Grandeur* and joined them now. Valerie introduced them all to Mej, Lien, and the assembled Lavkins. She didn't give any other details as to why they had come, and the Lavkins didn't ask for any. They were too busy staring at Kalan in awe.

"Wait, you said 'squadron,'" Robin said. "Does that mean this isn't the entire fleet?"

Titters of laugher went through the gathered crowd.

"No, not hardly," Mej said. "Most of the squadrons are

spread throughout the system and beyond, even, doing what they can to fight for the greater good."

"And why aren't you?" Valerie asked.

Some might have considered the question blunt, but Mej and Lien didn't seem to mind in the least. "It's because Lolack isn't here. He's our leader, and my brother. We can't and won't leave without him."

Kalan thought about that a moment. "From the information we got, you all arrived here five years ago. Have you been waiting for him to return this whole time?"

"Yes," Lien said, "and it hasn't been easy. We selected Rewot because it's so sparsely populated. There's a race of island-dwelling beings, but they are so spread out that we've had almost no contact with them. Rewot has presented some challenges, though. As your scanner probably told you, there isn't much land. We had to rig our ships to float, and we've been living in them for years."

"The weather is another concern," Mej explained. "Hurricanes are incredibly frequent. Our ships are strong enough to withstand even the most violent of them, but that doesn't make them fun."

"So why stay here?" Flynn asked. "Why not just wait in orbit for your leader to return."

"Resources," Mej said. "The benefits outweigh the costs. Rewot has plentiful sea life, as well as edible underwater plants. There's more food here than we would ever need, all free for the taking."

Valerie scratched her ear. Kalan could tell she was starting to get impatient.

"We need to talk to you about why we're here," she said.

Lien smiled and gestured to Kalan. "Yes. You've brought

us a Grayhewn. Thank you so much. Now our great alliance can resume."

"That's not the only reason," Valerie said. "We believe you're in danger."

"Danger?" Mej asked. "From what?" Then she held up a hand. "Actually, don't tell me—not yet. The crowd here is very anxious to hear the results of the testing. Isn't that right?"

The gathered Lavkins let out a cheer that made it clear they were indeed excited for the results.

"So here's what I propose," she continued. "I handle the military affairs for this squadron. Why don't you and your friends come with me, and you can tell me about this threat. Lien handles matters related to lore and history, so he can take Kalan to perform the testing."

"Uh, hang on," Kalan said. "Testing?"

Lien waved a hand as if shooing away a silly notion. "Don't worry, it's just a simple examination. Nothing to be afraid of." He paused thinking. "Well, until the second stage, anyway. But that won't be until tomorrow at the earliest."

"Er, okay," Kalan said.

The crowd let out a cheer, their impossibly thin arms waving rhythmically in the air.

Lien took Kalan by the arm and lead him away.

CHAPTER FIVE

Walking with Mej, Valerie felt like a child. These Lavkins even carried themselves in a way that felt more adult, though maybe that had to do with their military nature and all they had been through. One didn't become part of a legendary fleet of badasses without having been through a situation or two.

"You...lead this ship?" Mej asked, gesturing to the *Grandeur*. "How is that possible, considering the presence of the Bandian?"

"That's a long story," Valerie answered, glancing around at the beautiful island and the large ships nearby. "Something tells me we have time, though. Am I wrong?"

"Come, let me show you my brother's ship," Mej replied as an answer. "If you've come all this way, you must have a reason. I would like to understand all of it."

They walked to the largest ship there...what back on Earth would have passed for a whole city, with a walkway connecting it to the island. The turrets on the top dwarfed anything Valerie had seen up to now, even those she had fought against on the space station where she had learned of Talrok's betrayal. Well, that he wasn't the real Talrok, anyway.

"The stories this ship could tell if it had a life of its own," Mej said, walking with her hands behind her and looking up at the ship in awe.

"Let's hope it doesn't come to that," Valerie said.

"Indeed. Do you know that we once faced down the five best ships in the Skulla armada with only this one vessel? But now Lolack is gone, his second-in-command is gone... and the ship just sits here, as if all of those adventures were some nearly-forgotten dream."

"You were part of these battles?" Valerie asked.

Mej nodded. "I rode at my brother's side. That's how we do it—a family crews each vessel. It isn't easy, you know. None of it is in warfare, but we do what we must to survive, and to make the universe a safer place."

"And my story?" Valerie asked. "Hearing it...that's to judge whether I'm on the good side or not?"

Mej smiled, though not with her eyes. "You're a smart one, at least. You see, even if your friend back there is a true Bandian, we don't know what that makes *you*. You could be holding him hostage. Maybe you're blackmailing him, or even tricking him. Duping him into something without him knowing."

"I promise you that none of those are true."

"I want to believe you, but..." They reached the ramp to the ship and ascended it. "It's not easy, as you well know, being in charge of so many. Putting trust where it doesn't belong can be very risky."

"And failing to put trust where it *does* belong can be just as risky."

"Like I said, a smart one," Mej said. They walked on in silence until they reached the hatch, and she gestured for Valerie to enter first.

Valerie paused, looking at her. "If you are fighting for the right kind of justice, then we'll get along fine. I'll tell you my story, and we'll see how this works out for both of us."

"I test you, you test me." Mej smiled, then ducked in first. "Naturally."

The inside of the ship wasn't anything like Valerie had expected from what she'd seen with Bad Company. Here was more glory and chaos—statues, tapestries, and other forms of art to symbolize the great warriors who had served in this ship. The walls were smooth metal, refined to have that perfect military shine that the Lost Fleet crew still wore five years after being grounded here.

Mej led her to an office that overlooked much of the ship. Large, with a view out into space—clearly the admiral's quarters.

"My brother," Mej started, "was the bravest Lavkin I've ever seen. Selfless, too. He gave it all up to serve, and I can't tell you how many times he ran into battle with no thoughts about his own safety, just his crew's. Something about the look in your eyes makes me feel the same about you, though it could be good or bad in your case."

"Is that so?"

"You tell me." Mej gestured to a seat on near side of the admiral's desk, then took the main chair for herself. "Do you start fires, or put them out?"

"That depends. If the wood is twisted and gnarled, or deformed to the point that it hurts others? I'll burn the shit out of that. I see a fire about to singe a kitten's tail? Call me 'Ms. Firewoman.'"

Mej cocked her head, analyzing her. "You talk funny, but I like it. So...tell me how you came to be in business with the Bandian."

Valerie sighed. "Where do I begin?"

The Lavkin leaned forward, elbows on the table, and folded her hands. "How about the day you were made a vampire? Is it like they say? Did you miss the sunrise most of all?"

"You know something about vampires?"

"I've done some research, although only from what the tech gurus could hack from your networks. Sorry."

"Ah, you *think* you know about vampires, then." She leaned in now too, smiling. "You have no idea."

There was nothing to lose by sharing her story here, so she did. She started with that day in Old France when she realized she would never see her parents again, and the cravings for blood. She told Mej how she'd realized her vampire brother was wrong, that hurting innocents could no longer be allowed, and how she had eventually risen to be Michael's Justice Enforcer. And the story went on, Mej's eyes grew wider and wider with disbelief and awe.

Finally Valerie brought the story to a close, leaving Mej momentarily speechless.

"So," Valerie asked, smiling, "was that the sort of vampire you had in mind?"

Mej laughed, then laughed louder. "I like you, Justice Enforcer."

"Ah, I'm trying out something, actually. Since I'm in space and all, what do you think about 'Prime Enforcer?'"

"Ohh, I love that!" Mej considered her, then shook her head in awe once more. "And I love that every word you spoke was true. I have a knack for this. Might have left out some details, but I'll let that slide.

"Not everyone wants to know all the details," Valerie replied with a wink. Now she leaned in. "Your turn."

"My turn?"

Valerie nodded. "We believe the leader of the Lost Fleet is being targeted. All of you really, but principally him. A powerful AI is searching for him, but we mean to find him first."

"My brother..." Mej shook her head. "He's been a hard man to find."

She spun and opened a panel on the back wall, revealing a glowing map of what they knew of the universe. It didn't coincide much with the map that the Etheric Federation had of the universe. It showed more, so much more that it was overwhelming just looking at it.

"We're here," Mej said, indicating a nearby section that glowed as she pointed at it. "My brother wouldn't have gone far, but that doesn't mean he isn't in hiding." She pointed to a small dot nearby. "Here's where he often went with the boys to blow off steam. We've sent Lavkins out there from time to time to look out for him. Even had a rotating shift for the first year, but no luck. I tried going home once to that firestorm of a planet we were raised on, but no luck there either."

"Your home planet and his... It isn't far from here?"

"That's correct." Mej lit up a planet on the map. "But

like I said, no luck there. It's largely uninhabited, and there are storms galore."

"I see…" Valerie stood, nodding her thanks. "Then it seems our best bet is start with the space station. We can ask around and see if we learn something."

"The minute you do, please let me know." Mej stood and gestured to the door. "Come, I'll show you more of the ship before we head back."

"I would like that," Valerie replied with a smile, and they made their way out. Although they'd arrived with tension and suspicion, they were leaving as allies in a war against evil and injustice.

CHAPTER SIX

Lien directed Kalan toward a metal causeway that led off the island and onto one of the ships.

"So when you say this is going to be an examination," Kalan said, "are you talking about a written test? I've never been much of a test-taker. One look at a multiple-choice question and the page goes blurry."

"Do they have a lot of multiple choice tests on SEDE?" Lien asked. Then he chuckled. "I'm sorry if that's too personal. I noticed the tattoos on your arm. SEDE's reputation is far-reaching."

Kalan shook his head. "Man, even on a strange planet I'm labeled an ex-convict."

"I'm not judging," the Lavkin quickly responded. "I know what those tattoos mean. You were born there, not sent there for committing a crime. And even if you had been sent there I wouldn't hold it against you. People make mistakes."

"That's very open-minded of you."

Lien chuckled. "Maybe all these years of open seas and open skies have made me open my mind a bit."

They reached the end of the causeway and stepped onto a mid-size ship. It rocked gently under Kalan's feet, and his first few steps were a bit shaky.

"That'll get better shortly," Lien said when he noted Kalan's unsteady walk. He gestured to the ship around them. "Welcome to *Flamebird*."

"It's beautiful," Kalan said. He meant it, too. The moment he had walked through the airlock, he noticed the elegant design. The bulkheads rose at dramatic angles, and every surface was decorated with intricate but tasteful etchings.

"Thank you," Lien said. "It's been in my family for generations."

That gave Kalan pause. "Your family? I thought this was a military fleet."

"Oh, it is, but in our culture whole families join the fleet together. We believe family is important, so we make it part of almost everything we do. Every ship is run by a family, or a group of families. They live, work, and fight aboard the ship. That way if a battle does come, they aren't just defending their ship, they're defending their family and their home."

"Sounds kind of messed up to me," Wearl said.

Kalan almost jumped. He'd had no idea the Shimmer was behind him.

As if reading his thoughts, Wearl said, "Oh, come on. Did you really think I was going to let you go all alone to some mysterious 'testing' with a stranger? You must be as crazy as you are beautiful."

He suppressed the urge to question her on that choice of adjective. As they often had when going into unfamiliar situations, they'd decided to keep her existence a secret for now. It paid to have an invisible team member only you and your people could hear.

"Anyway," Lien continued, "it can get a little complicated. My family had this ship, and Mej's family had another. When we married, my siblings took over this ship and I moved to hers. It's much bigger. I do still come here to do research, though. The medical facilities are top-notch. Ah, here we are."

He opened a door and led Kalan inside.

Kalan had never been in a research laboratory, but if you'd asked him to imagine what one looked like it probably would been something close to the room he stood in now. Huge machines with weird arms and tubes coming from them lined the walls, waiting to serve mysterious functions. A wall of computer monitors stood at one end of the room. There was even a table with some test tubes on a stand.

Lien took a seat at a desk near the front of the room and gestured for Kalan to sit across from him. "I didn't answer your question before."

"What question?" Kalan asked as he slid into the seat. It had clearly been designed for Lavkins, so it was far too narrow for him. He had to keep both feet firmly planted on the deck to avoid teetering off the thing.

"About the test. You asked if it was a written exam. It's actually a series of medical tests."

Kalan paused for a moment before answering. "I'm suddenly less excited about this."

"It's nothing invasive," Lien said with a laugh. "No reason to be nervous."

"Yeah," Wearl said, "that was probably what they told Willom, too—right before they turned him into a freaking cyborg."

"I'm going to need a little more information before I let you run me through any machines or poke me with any needles," Kalan told him. "We did just meet, after all."

Lien nodded. "Totally understandable. We have to make sure you really are a Bandian."

Kalan chuckled at that. "The gray skin and large frame don't give me away?"

"There are ways to fake such things."

"If you think I'm a Pallicon—"

"That's one of the possibilities we'll test for," Lien said," but only one. My family has overseen Lavkin lore and history for many generations, and we have protocols for the tests we need to run if a Bandian should appear. It may seem strange, but the alliance we made with your people is our most sacred. There are those in the galaxy who would take advantage of the situation."

Kalan considered that for a moment. On the one hand, it was insane to let a person he had just met and had no reason to trust perform some sort of medical test on him. On the other hand, there was something about these Lavkins that felt...right. He trusted them, though he knew he probably shouldn't yet.

Wearl had said the way they worked their ships as a family was messed up, but Kalan didn't agree. To him, it was surprisingly touching. Thinking about the same family living, dying, fighting, and working on this ship generation after generation...there was a beauty to it. He imagined children learning about the ship at their grandparents' knees, and one day teaching their own grandchildren those same lessons.

Maybe it was because Kalan didn't have much of a family himself. It had just been him and his mother as far back as he could remember. His mother was locked up on SEDE and he was out now, so he'd never see her again.

He knew that was part of what was driving his quest to find other Bandians, and that it was affecting his judgment now. But he didn't care. He felt a tingle of emotion at the way these Lavkins put family before all else.

"Okay," Kalan said. "Let's begin."

"Good." Lien spun his chair around and dug through a drawer for a minute. "Ah, here it is."

He opened a case and pulled out a syringe wrapped in plastic. "This test is simple. Give me your hand. It's just a tiny prick."

Kalan expected Wearl to make a joke about that turn of phrase, but she didn't.

Instead she said, "Kalan, are you sure you want to do this?"

In response, Kalan held out his hand.

Lien watched the hand for a few moments. Kalan assumed he was looking for the telltale flicker around the edges that happened when Pallicons were shapeshifting. "Good. Now the prick."

Quick as a burst of light, Lien poked the needle into Kalan's index finger. Then he inserted it in a slot next to the computer and tapped the screen repeatedly, his fingers hitting commands too quickly for Kalan to follow.

"Easy as that," Lien said, turning back toward Kalan. "It'll take a few minutes to run the protocol, then we'll have our results. While we're waiting, why don't you tell me what you know about the Lavkins and our Lost Fleet."

Kalan shrugged. "Honestly, before last month I'd never heard of you."

"That's a shame," Lien said with a frown. "Then I take it you don't know how our two peoples came together and aligned their causes?"

Kalan shook his head. He didn't know much of anything about the history of the Bandians, let alone the archaic details of their treaties.

"It started out oddly," Lien said. "We attacked a settlement of Skulla, although the details of what caused that skirmish are lost to time. Perhaps they'd slighted us in some way, or perhaps we were greedy for more land. Either way, we attacked, and the Skulla mounted a rather pathetic defense."

"Not sure what any of this has to do with the Bandians," Wearl said with a sigh.

"What we didn't know," Lien continued, "was that the Skulla on that planet had a treaty with the Bandians. Our attacking force was a thousand strong, but a group of one hundred Bandians fearlessly joined the fight nonetheless. And to our surprise, they managed to turn the tide of the battle. They used brilliant—and perhaps reckless—strategies we'd never seen before. They defended the Skulla with such ferocity! We'd seen people defend their homes like that, but to put it all on the line for an ally truly impressed our fleet. We knew we wanted to work with these beings."

"I can't imagine they were too thrilled to work with you after you'd just attacked their friends," Kalan pointed out.

Lien chuckled. "Indeed they weren't. It took time to build trust between us. Decades. But eventually we proved we could be loyal friends to them, just as they were to the Skulla, and the alliance was formed."

Kalan looked the Lavkin in the eyes. "So why is your fleet is still around, and the Bandians are not?"

Lien looked at the ground. "It was our greatest failure, and the reason we spread out—many of us went into hiding. We weren't there when the Bandians needed us most. When they were being hunted."

"By whom?"

Lien looked up in surprise. "You don't know?"

Kalan shook his head. "My mother didn't know much about the history of our people. She was an orphan."

Lien scratched his chin with his impossibly long fingers. "Have you heard of the Wandarby? They're a cult of religious Pallicons who believe the Bandians are an abomination that must be destroyed."

"I've heard of the cult, but I didn't know their name. Honestly, I didn't know if they were real."

Lien's face tightened in anger at the thought of the Wandarby. "Oh, they're real. They hunted the Bandians to near-extinction, and when that was done they turned their attention to us, the Bandians' greatest allies."

Kalan didn't react visibly to the news, but his mind was reeling. This Pallicon cult was the reason his people were gone? When he'd heard of the cult, he'd imagined a few dozen Pallicons gathered in a house somewhere talking about the evils of the Bandians. This had to be much bigger.

And now they were coming after the Lavkins simply because of their association with the Bandians?

"The Wandarby cultists are brutal fighters," Lien continued. "Our best defenses against them have always been our mobility and superior flying skills. A few months ago a group of Wandarby scouts discovered our location, and they've been attacking us ever since. Small strikes designed to frighten us, but Mej believes they are planning a much bigger attack."

"Why not go somewhere else?"

"We cannot," Lien said with a smile. "Remember what I said about family? Our admiral is family to everyone in the squadron. To even suggest leaving without him would be insulting, and no one in the fleet would consider it."

Something beeped, and Lien turned back to the screen. "Ah, the results!" After studying them for a moment, he turned back to Kalan. "Congratulations, my friend. You are a full-blooded Bandian, which makes you and me allies."

Lien held out his hand and Kalan grabbed it, shaking it to the left and the right in the Vurugu style.

"Let's go tell the others the good news," the Lavkin said.

When they had made it back to the island, Mej, Valerie, and the others were already waiting for them.

"How'd the test go, Kalan?" Robin asked with a grin. "Did you pass?"

The Lavkins waited for the answer with wide eyes, anticipation clear on their face.

Lien stepped forward. "My friends, we have a verified Bandian standing in our midst."

A riotous cheer went up from the crowd.

Jilla sidled up next to Kalan and leaned in close. "Don't let all this go to your head. I remember when you were just a shy, nerdy kid on the cellblock."

"Don't worry. This isn't about me, it's about the Lavkins. They blame themselves for the Bandians being wiped out. In me, they see a chance to make up for their mistake."

The cheers finally died down a little, and Valerie marched up to him. "This is exciting and all, but we need to go."

Kalan raised an eyebrow in surprise. "Go where?"

"From what Mej told me, they won't leave this spot without their leader. I believe if we find him and the other heroes who left with him, we can unite the fleet. If we can do that we'll have the firepower to defeat Aranaught, and maybe even win a powerful new ally for the Etheric Federation."

Kalan considered her plan. It made sense, and it was the best move for the Prime Enforcer, but it didn't feel right for him.

"Valerie, I need to stay here," he told her.

"What? Why? You like the way they worship you?"

He blushed a little at that. "Not at all."

"Then why?"

He took a deep breath, trying to figure out how to put words to the feeling in his heart. "I guess I feel responsible for their safety. We know Aranaught is after them. Lien told me a Pallicon cult has been harassing them, too. I won't leave them to face that alone. They had an alliance with my people, so I guess that means they have an alliance with me."

After a moment, Valerie nodded. "I can respect that. We'll go find this Lolack guy, and you'll make sure they're still alive when we get back with him. Then we will reunite the fleet."

"I'm staying with Kalan," Wearl said quickly.

"Obviously," Valerie said with a smile. "Kalan, I assume you want Jilla, too?"

"Wouldn't hurt."

"Okay, but that means you're taking Bob again."

Kalan chuckled. "I wouldn't have it any other way."

The teams wished each other luck on their respective missions and said their goodbyes. Kalan didn't know how Valerie was going to find Lolack in the vast expanse of this system, but if anyone could do it, it was her and her Elites.

Within the hour the *Singlaxian Grandeur* lifted off from the island, and soon it had disappeared into the evening sky.

CHAPTER SEVEN

Checks and security at the space station were a joke, but after they had docked and exited the ship to get a look around, they saw why. Everyone here had a gun, and everyone here seemed drunk. It was practically a free-for-all, the exception being several blue-skinned people like Arlay who were walking about with large body guards who had marbled skin of black and gray.

"A family reunion?" Flynn asked, giddy because he didn't have to watch the ship for once.

Arlay frowned and looked like she was about to hit him. "My people...they've sort of chosen a different path than I did. They're mostly pirates."

"Oh, damn," Robin said, glancing back, then taking a stutter-step to remain close to the group.

"If anyone's making money here, they're likely behind it."

"And if anyone's causing trouble it's likely them too?" Valerie asked, wishing she had Kalan and Bob and the rest here to help deal with any situation that might arise.

Arlay nodded.

"But not you?" Garcia asked, glancing back at her. "Hey, I have to ask."

"No, you don't," Robin said, smacking him on the back of the head playfully.

"It's okay, and no, not me. The thought never crossed my mind. I had...other dreams."

"Such as?" Garcia asked, turning make sure Robin wasn't going to hit him this time.

"Other dreams," Arlay said, not giving away anything more this time.

Garcia let it rest, and was the first to enter the bar portion of the space station, where they hoped to find their answers. What they found was a scene out of a circus, as far as Valerie was concerned. Male and female blue aliens with tentacled hair were dancing at tables, sparsely dressed, and all manner of others were either watching or drinking at their own tables. Two Lavkins sat at one side, and Valerie nodded their way.

"Could they be members of the Lost Fleet?" she asked, and since nobody made any protests, she walked over to them and introduced herself.

"We're looking for a man named Lolack," she started, but the two stopped her with looks saying, "Here we go again."

"You won't get far asking about him around here," one of the Lavkins said. "Do you know how long that search went on, and how many times others have come through here asking?"

"However," the second added, "you're the first human female on his trail, so what're you having?"

"Are you hitting on me?" she asked, not totally sure.

"I think he was," Garcia said, moving over to them. One of the Lavkins started to stand, but Valerie grabbed Garcia's arm and walked back to the others.

"What're we trying to accomplish here, exactly?" Robin asked, having witnessed the whole charade. "You said so yourself, and they just confirmed it—this isn't a lead. Not anymore."

"How about a little rest and relaxation then?" Flynn asked, watching two semi-attractive Skulla walk by.

"Don't tell me you're into this?" Garcia asked him with a laugh.

"Hey, I don't know." Flynn shrugged. "A man's got needs, and something about those tattoos…"

Garcia laughed, but the others weren't sure what they thought about that.

"Come on," Valerie said, motioning them toward the bar. "We'll get a round and try to figure this out. Arlay, maybe you'd have better luck ordering here?"

Arlay nodded, still very clearly not comfortable here. They had the money from Tol, so they didn't have to worry about cost. She got a bottle of a strange blue liquid that went down smoothly and they gathered around a table in the corner, trying to ignore the dancers. Well, everyone except Flynn did. He was apparently into them, too.

"Flynn's in heat," Robin said with a laugh, "so the rest of us need to figure this out. What, we're going to come out here and find him on Day One, when the entire Lost Fleet couldn't?"

Valerie took a sip and felt her throat go semi-numb as it went down, then let the shivers run their course. She told the others what Mej had told her, going back through the details, but nobody could make anything of it.

"Keep asking around," she said finally. "Maybe we can put pieces together where others couldn't."

"Or someone will talk to us where they wouldn't talk to the Lost Fleet," Arlay said. "They do have a reputation here, after all."

"On it," Flynn said, standing and smiling at the two Skulla from earlier. They giggled and didn't turn away when he headed over.

"I'd like to say that's the attitude," Valerie said, "but I'm not sure it is."

The others laughed and agreed to split up and start conversations. Valerie made her way around the room. After a couple hours, and they were on the point of exhaustion. Valerie started to head for the floor, pausing in utter confusion as one of the blue men started dancing nearby while eyeing her. As nice as his abs were she wasn't interested, and didn't see how she could get past the blue skin and tentacles even if she had been.

"Excuse me," she said, starting to inch away.

"Lolack, right?" he asked.

"You know something?"

He smiled, moving her way while still waving his hips from side to side in a way others here must've found alluring but she found comical. He saw the look in her eyes and sighed, then nodded toward Arlay.

"You know who she is, don't you?"

"She came with me, so…" Valerie glanced at Arlay, who stood not far from Garcia, chatting up one of her kind.

"Well, if *she* doesn't know, none of us will." The male

gave her one last wishful glance, then moved on to dance for someone else.

Valerie continued around the room, debating her next move and wondering about Arlay. Of course she had been involved with all this, but could she be holding back?

The last thing Valerie wanted to do was sew doubt and mistrust among her team, so she walked straight up to her newest teammate and asked, "You have an idea where he is?"

Arlay glanced around nervously, then nodded. "I've been trying to figure it out, actually."

"Explain."

"He used to talk about his people. About how some of them lived in more primitive ways, and how he fought for them so that they might have a better life." Arlay held her hand up, considering, and then drew an imaginary map on her palm. "If this wasn't his home planet—which I don't think it was, although the description sounded similar— maybe it's not far off?"

"So we're looking for a planet with similar weather patterns and whatnot?"

"Exactly." Arlay glanced around. "Problem is, most of these patrons aren't from around here. They come in, party, and go back to their daily troubles."

"And if we went back to ask Mej?" Valerie asked.

"Not likely. If she had an inkling about this place, she would've said so."

"Right." Valerie ran a hand through her hair, pausing as the blue male passing by clearly checked her out. "Well, keep it up. Maybe we can find something."

As the hours droned on, it became clear the crowd

wasn't changing. More ships would arrive eventually, but there was no reason to believe their passengers would know anything more than these. At one point Valerie caught a glimpse of Flynn exiting with a tall Lavkin and a short Skulla, but decided they could allow themselves some fun rather than wallowing in despair at their first big roadblock. She even started to dance when the blue male came up to her for the twentieth time, Robin laughing at her side as she too rocked her hips from side to side.

Surprisingly no fights started, although at one point one of the marble-skinned guards bumped into Garcia. He had words for the tall beast, but backed off at a look from Valerie. That earned her group more looks of curiosity, but nothing new in terms of the mission.

"You're so advanced in your sexuality, right?" Robin asked, leaning in to Valerie, then motioning to the blue male. "Well, there you go."

"I-I…"

"Wow, actually caught you off balance," Robin said with a laugh. "Scared you'll wake up looking like a blueberry? Come on, we need to set an example for the universe."

She stepped between Valerie and the blue male, taking his hands and moving with him to the rhythmic music. Turning so that he was between the two women, Robin moved him back to where he was brushing against Valerie with each move.

"Robin," she growled in frustration.

"Come on, show us how free with all this you are," Robin replied, then pulled the male close and kissed him.

Valerie hadn't thought it would bother her so much, but seeing that sent a shudder of irritation through her. She pushed her way past the two and out into the hallway, figuring she'd make her way back to the *Grandeur*.

However, halfway there a Lavkin female stepped out of the shadows.

"You...you came with the one who calls himself Big Papa?" she asked.

"What?" Valerie frowned, about to sidestep her.

"The one you came with—tall, muscular?"

Valerie took a second to process this. "You mean Flynn, not Big Papa."

"Right, well, beside the point." The Lavkin female tried to hide a smile at that, but returned to business. "He told me what you are asking about, and I left a planet that meets your description. Left it long ago, but it's still there."

"What planet?"

She smiled and said, "I gave the coordinates to Big Papa so you can check it out. I wanted to be sure to tell you too, though, because he's a tad distracted."

"Oh." Valerie frowned, then said, "*Oh*! He's with the Skulla?"

"As far as I know."

"I'm sorry." Valerie tried to come up with a way to explain Earth men, but the Lavkin held up a hand to stop her.

"Don't be. I got mine, and believe me...Big Papa deserves the name."

"Oh, God," Valerie said, wishing she could wipe that information from her mind. "Can we just... Tell me how to find this place."

The Lavkin laughed and told her before returning to the music.

They had a destination, and Valerie was eager to get on with the mission.

However, Robin and the blue male were still dancing, Garcia and a couple of tough-looking blue pirates were going shot for shot with the drinks, and Flynn was still having his fun.

She could give them a few more minutes, at least. Instead of lingering in the bar, though, she made her way to the walkways on the other side and strolled down some of them, looking out at the stars and depths of space.

These passageways were floor and window and not much else. They existed for strolls such as this, perfect for gazing at all the excitement of the universe. What was the Colonel up to at this moment, or BA and Michael? And how could any evil stand against them?

In a universe this expansive, it seemed impossible that they would be able to manage it all. There were probably beings out there even stronger than them. Given the vampires and Weres on Earth, what horrors hid in the darkest corners of the universe?

At that moment, anything was possible.

Thinking about Earth sent a wave of nostalgia through her, and she closed her eyes as her hands clutched the cold metal railing between her and the windows into space. She ignored the noise around her to remember an interlude with her friend Sandra—before she had completely settled in with Diego, before the child. The memory of the two of them sitting in Sandra's place sharing a glass of wine was a distant dream; a moment that might have never happened.

And yet, that life seemed so much more real than this. Here she was, in a planetary system she hadn't known existed back then. Her friends were messing around with aliens, and they were all about to fly off to some random planet in search of a tall orange alien legend.

She wished there was a way to write to Sandra and tell her all about this. That was the first thing she would ask Nathan or Michael about when this whole situation had been dealt with. She needed a way to hear from them, to know they were okay.

"Val?" Flynn asked. The Skulla female was at his side.

Apparently she had wanted to show him the views from out here.

"Are you... I mean, is everything okay?" He glanced at her, clearly ready to end his little romance to talk with her if needed.

"Enjoy yourselves," she said, smiling at them. "I'm just taking a moment to myself before we head out."

"So soon?" the Skulla asked.

Flynn shrugged and turned to Valerie, hopeful.

While Aranaught was out there, this whole thing with receiving the planet's coordinates from some random female in a bar was a bit of a stretch.

"Take your time," Valerie said. "I'll walk the perimeter, then we'll get on our way."

"Roger that," he said, and she heard the two whispering about not wasting the time staring out into space when they could be having some real fun. They walked off, giggling.

This was a new life, Valerie reminded herself. She hoped that she too could relax and enjoy it someday, and swore to make an effort after this mission.

CHAPTER EIGHT

Kalan and his friends spent the next few days getting acclimated to the life in the Lavkin colony. They were assigned to *Flamebird*, Lien's family's ship. It was the least populated, and for Lien it was a point of personal pride that these honored guests were staying there.

Their quarters were a bit smaller than on the *Grandeur*, and it was clear they'd been designed for the long willowy bodies of the Lavkins. Kalan had to sleep on his side and lie as still as he could, and even then he still toppled out of the bunk two or three times a night.

It was even worse for Jilla and Wearl. Since the Lavkins didn't know Wearl existed, they hadn't provided her a bunk. The Shimmer had kindly offered to share quarters with Kalan, but he'd quickly declined. She was rooming with Jilla and bedding down on the floor, and she was none too happy about the situation.

Still, it wasn't all bad. There was a whole new digital library for Kalan to peruse, and he was learning a lot about the history of both the Lavkins and the Bandians. There was a breathtaking sunrise and sunset every night, and they had wonderful views of both from the observation deck at the top of the ship. And then there were the Lavkins themselves, who were kind and welcoming to all of them, even Jilla. She'd been a bit worried that they'd hold her Pallicon heritage against her, but no one so much as mentioned it.

Their days were spent fishing, chatting with various Lavkins, and preparing meals from the delicious and slightly sweet flesh of the fish of Rewot.

Kalan was surprised at how important family was to these people. It went far beyond simply living and working on the same ship. Even when they were out fishing, the family groups tended to stick together. When they did mingle with others they did so as a family, one group approaching and merging with the other so various people could spend time together.

"It's a miracle they ever mate, considering that their parents and aunts and uncles are always around," Jilla observed one day while they were sitting near the shore on the island. "Doesn't exactly set the mood from romance."

"It's bizarre, is what it is," Wearl said. "Children should be able to wander and forge their own lives. Their parents are stifling them."

Kalan understood where she was coming from. In the Shimmers' culture each child had only one parent, who was randomly assigned by the government. Still, there was something about the whole arrangement here on Rewot that he found charming. "I don't know, Wearl... It's not like the parents are forcing them to stay nearby. The kids all seem to be having a great time."

Jilla punched him lightly on the arm. "Oh come on, admit it. If you were one of those kids, this would drive you crazy. Back when we were teenagers, you couldn't wait to get away from our moms and spend time with me alone."

"I'm not going to argue with that," Kalan said with a chuckle. "But I will say this: judging this culture against what we'd prefer is probably a mistake. They have their own way of life, and we have to respect that."

"I still say it's weird," Wearl told him.

The next day, Mej took them out on a long flat boat with a motor hanging off the back of it. When they were all on board, she reached down and touched the engine. The faint glow the Lavkins' skin always had intensified, and the motor sprang to life.

Kalan had seen a few such displays during his time on Rewot. Apparently the Lavkins' skin had a conductive quality that allowed them to spark machines to life. Many were built without any type of starting mechanism, including their ships—which had the added benefit of allowing only Lavkins to operate their ships and other machines.

Once the motor started, Mej piloted them through the maze of floating ships to an area Kalan had never seen before. She guided them around one of the larger ships and pulled them to a stop near another hunk of metal—the burned-out hull of a Lavkin ship.

It was difficult to imagine what could have destroyed such a powerful ship so completely.

"I wanted to show you a little of the Wandarby cult's handiwork," Mej announced.

Kalan's eyes widened. The Pallicon cult had done this? They were more powerful than he'd imagined if they were capable of this type of devastation.

"They strike hard and fast," the Lavkin explained, "and they're focused. They don't attack with the intention of killing us all or defeating us completely. They concentrate all their efforts and firepower on a single ship. We never know which one, though, so we are forced to spread out. When we discover which ship they're targeting we shift our defenses, and sometimes it's enough to fight them off. Other times..." Her voice trailed off and she gestured toward the hulk.

Kalan let out a low whistle. He could only imagine that type of attack. The enemy swooped in, fired everything they had at a single vessel, then flew away.

"They're highly motivated, too," Mej continued. "The Wandarby take a vow not to change shapes until they've killed their first Lavkin or Bandian."

Jilla shook her head in disbelief. "Wow, that's quite the sacrifice for a Pallicon. Shapeshifting is considered an essential part of life."

Mej sighed sadly. "Yes, so you understand how much they'd have to hate us to give that up."

That night back on *Flamebird*, Jilla, Wearl, and Kalan gathered in Kalan's quarters to discuss what they'd learned.

"Strategically it's a tough situation," Jilla said. "Our enemies strike from the sky. They move fast, and know exactly where we will be. We can't move or fly the ships because they've been rigged to float. Lien told me it would take weeks of work to make the ships flight-ready again. And we don't know which ship they'll target, or when."

"Hmm," Bob said. "What if we *did* know which ship they were going to target?"

"That would be great," Kalan said. "Any idea how we can make that happen?"

Bob scratched his chin pensively. "Well, we do have an invisible Shimmer and an actual Pallicon on our team."

"You're suggesting Wearl and I infiltrate the Wandarby?" Jilla asked. "That's actually a pretty good idea, Bob."

Even Bob looked surprised. "Wow, thanks."

Kalan wasn't so sure. "It's too dangerous. We don't know much about the Wandarby cult aside from what we've heard from the Lavkins."

"Still," Wearl said, "it seems like it could be too good of an idea to pass up."

Kalan wasn't convinced. "Maybe, if we see an opportunity to make it happen, but it seems like a long shot. How would we even get you aboard their ships? Wouldn't they immediately know you didn't belong there?"

Jilla patted Bob on the shoulder. "Seems like Kalan has shot you down for now, but keep those ideas coming."

"Sorry, Bob," Kalan said. "For now, our best option is to do what we can to help the Lavkins fight if the Pallicons do attack. Until then, let's get to know our hosts and enjoy our time here."

As he finished speaking, there was a knock on the door. He opened it to find Lien standing on the other side. "Remember when I told you there was another part to the test? Well, the time has come. Would you be so kind as to follow me?"

Kalan cocked a thumb toward his friends. "Can they come along?"

Lien looked surprised. "Of course. I'd be offended if they didn't. The whole squadron will be there."

"Great," Kalan said. "I'm not going to have to make a speech, am I?"

"Nothing like that," Lien said. "This is going to be a whole different type of show."

As they walked through the ship, Lien explained further.

"The nature of this test necessitates that I not tell you very much about it before we begin. I *can* tell you that you will be in no physical danger, but some participants find it upsetting. The test is designed to reveal your true reactions in extreme circumstances, and seeing the truth about ourselves can sometimes be unpleasant."

"You're really selling it here, Lien," Jilla said with a laugh.

"It's important that I be as truthful as possible," he replied. "Two more things. First, you are by no means required to take the test. It's entirely up to you. Second, every Lavkin takes this test. It's sort of a rite of passage."

"Why have me take it?" Kalan asked.

"Honestly? At the height of our alliance Bandians would regularly take the test, and they were known for their very high scores. In fact, a Bandian holds the all-time record. The best I've ever seen anyone score is eighty-two out of one hundred. I'm wondering if you can beat it. That would be amazing to see."

"No pressure," Wearl said dryly.

"Okay," Kalan said. "Let's do this thing."

They walked up the metal causeway toward the island. Just as they had been the day they'd arrived, most of the

Lavkins in the squadron were waiting. Unlike the first day, though, he now knew most of them. It felt much more intimidating to be in front of a gathering of people he knew and respected. There was a small machine about the size of his head sitting on a table in front of the crowd, as well as a chair and a large display screen.

As they stepped onto the island, the crowd went silent.

"They won't say a word during this entire process," Lien explained. "They don't want to risk distracting you." He motioned for Kalan to sit.

"Are you going to poke me with a needle again?"

"No." He picked up a small cup-like object that was attached to the machine by three thin wires. "This fits over your eye like a patch. Once I activate the machine, you will experience three scenarios. It will feel like you are there, and you will in fact forget that this is a test. That way we can gauge your true reactions."

Kalan's lips tightened into a thin line, but he nodded. "Okay. So it's imaginary, but I'll think it's real?"

"Exactly. And there's one more thing…everything you see will also be projected on this screen. That is the real point of this test—to see if you're willing to have your true reactions in intense situations laid bare for the entire squadron. Still want to go through with it?"

Kalan hesitated for a moment. He wanted nothing more than to have the acceptance of these Lavkins, but what if this test revealed something about his true character that they didn't like? He supposed that was the point of it all, though—to let them see his true self when his guard was down.

"Yeah, I am," he said.

"Good." Lien placed the cup-like device over his right eye. "Here we go." He touched the machine and his hand glowed briefly, and then—

Kalan stood in a garden of sorts. He didn't remember how he'd gotten there or how long he'd been there, but there was one urgent thought pulsing in his brain and refusing to be ignored: get out of there as quickly as possible.

He looked around, taking in his surroundings in more detail. Grass grew around his feet, and strange flowers he'd never seen before bloomed nearby. Around him was a ten-foot wall with a rounded top.

There was a sign mounted on top of the wall that read, **How quickly can you get out?**

He made his way down a grassy corridor until he came to a place where he either needed to turn right or left.

"I know what this is," he muttered to himself. "A damn maze."

If he wanted to get out of here quickly, he wasn't going to do it by solving the maze. He needed to get on top of that wall.

The first thing he tried was jumping and grabbing the top so he could haul himself up, but he discovered the top of the wall was slick. His fingers slipped off it every time he tried.

Next he tried pulling himself up by the ivy that covered some areas of the wall, but it tore loose and he crashed back to the ground.

He put his hands on his hips and took a deep breath. "Think your way out of this, Kalan. You can do it."

His eyes settled on the sign perched on top of the wall. If he had a rope or something to hook around that, he could pull himself up. He didn't have a rope, but he did have his shirt.

He quickly pulled off his shirt and stepped to the wall beneath the sign. Holding the shirt by each sleeve, he jumped as high as he could and swung the shirt up. On the third try he successfully hooked the shirt over the sign, then pulled himself to the top of the wall. Once he got past the curved edge, the wall was flat.

He stood up and surveyed the vast maze. When he saw all the dead ends, he was glad he hadn't tried to get through the maze. All he had to do now was walk along the edge wall and make three right turns, and he'd be out.

He started walking, and—

Kalan ran through the woods. Luckily it was a clear night, so the three moons in the sky lit his way. Once again he had no idea how he'd gotten here, but he knew he was being chased by a powerful enemy he had no chance of defeating. If they caught him, they'd kill him.

He dashed forward at top speed, leaping over logs and ducking under low-hanging branches. His lungs burned as he ran, and he felt a cramp forming in his left leg. Ignoring them both, he kept pushing onward.

After he'd been running for what felt like hours, he broke through the trees into an open grassy field. Joy surged in his chest, and he had the feeling he'd done it—he'd evaded his pursuers.

But when he saw what was in front of him, he jolted to a stop.

It was a ravine. In the moonlight he could see pretty far down, but he couldn't see the bottom. Far below the fog was thick, nullifying any chance he had of figuring out how deep the ravine really was.

His enemies were closing on him; he could feel it. If he jumped he would die, but at least it wouldn't give his enemies the satisfaction of killing him. He hesitated only a moment, then leaped into the ravine.

He hurtled down toward—

Kalan stood in a long hallway. The details of how he'd gotten here were once again hazy, but he completely understood his situation.

At the end of the hallway to his left stood a male he greatly admired, banging on the door to try to get out.

To his right were two males he greatly disliked, who were also pounding on a door on their end of the hallway. He knew these men weren't evil; he just didn't like them personally.

Kalan was holding a key in his hand...the key to both locked doors.

And on the floor in front of him was a bomb, its display counting down from eleven seconds.

Kalan knew he had time to make it to one of the doors,

saving himself and either the male he liked or the two he didn't.

Save one pleasant male, or two unpleasant ones? He needed to decide now or the chance would slip away.

It only took a moment for him to realize what he needed to do. He grabbed the key and threw it as hard as he could toward the two men. "Unlock the door!" he called to them.

One of the males nodded, scooped up the key, and did just that.

With three seconds left Kalan threw himself on top of the bomb, covering it with as much of his body as possible. He hoped it would be enough to save the male at the other end of the hallway.

One second left on the timer and—

———

Kalan was back on the island. He blinked hard, trying to get his bearings. The hot sun on his face, the feel of the chair under him, and the whisper of the breeze hitting the large screen brought him back to reality. He realized that everything he'd experienced was a simulation, but that didn't mean his heart wasn't racing. His face wasn't covered in sweat, too.

Lien removed the cup from his eye.

Kalan grinned up at him. "How'd I do?"

For a moment Lien's face was unreadable, then he broke out in a wide smile. "Eighty-seven. Best in my lifetime."

The crowd roared cheers and applauded.

He shakily stood up from his chair and put up a hand to calm the gathered Lavkins. He was a little embarrassed by the big deal they were making about all this.

When the cheering started to die down, Mej stepped forward and addressed the crowd. "Kalan proved his ability to think creatively in the maze. He proved his ability to act quickly and take decisive action in the ravine, and he proved his selfless heroism in the hallway with the bomb. My friends, I am proud to officially announce that we have a true Bandian in our midst. Not only biologically, but also in heart, mind, and soul."

The cheers started again and were even louder than before.

CHAPTER NINE

Walking onto this planet was like walking into a steamy bath. The journey from the space station had gone smoothly enough, and everyone was in a much better mood after their R&R.

But here it was hot and humid, and at the same time murky. The sky had a purple haze to it that made their surroundings difficult to discern. If not for the readings on the *Grandeur*, she would doubt there was a city directly ahead.

"Keep an eye out," Valerie told Garcia and Flynn. "You two are responsible for this ship."

"Nothing new there," Flynn replied with a grin. Arlay stood at his side, looking out at the planet as if curious but scared. It was best she stay back while Valerie and Robin explored, since the women could move at vampire speed if they had to.

"You're the ones going out into that," Garcia said with a hearty laugh. "I'll be surprised if I ever see you again, honestly."

"We have an invitation," Valerie said, smiling and patting her rifle.

Arlay appeared at the doorway with her helmet on and glanced around nervously. Considering her position of power back on the moon of Tol, she sure was cautious out here on worlds she hadn't traveled to before.

"Where do you need me?" Arlay asked.

Valerie thought about it, not sure how her kind would be accepted here. At least humans were mostly unknown, and therefore hadn't had time to make many enemies. Who knew what the inhabitants of this world would think of Arlay with her tentacled, dangling skin?

"Tell you what," Valerie said. "Maybe the three of you can defend the ship, but start doing scouting parties to see what else is around here?"

"You got it," Arlay replied, ducking back inside quickly.

"Eager, huh?" Robin said with a laugh.

"Are you super-excited to walk blindly into this?" Valerie replied, gesturing to their surroundings.

"We're not going blindly, not when the ship's sensors show the city in that direction." She pointed, but doubt was clearly visible in her eyes. All they could see was the haze, filled with looming shapes that could've been mountains or tall buildings.

"Let's find out," Valerie said with a wink, and took the lead. Robin shuffled up next to her a moment later, glancing around with trepidation.

"You know, when I first found out I'd be able to walk in the light again it was like taking that first breath after nearly drowning," Robin said. "And then...Then you took me to space. We've been traveling for over a month since Tol, and now this."

Valerie laughed. "You blame *me* for this?"

"Well, we could probably find justice to enforce on some island that's more of a tropical paradise, right? You think baddies only live on horrible, desolate shit-holes?"

"Good question." Valerie walked in silence, considering her question while trying to ignore a scent like overripe peaches that permeated the air here. "I think you could be right. Hell, that Pallicon place wasn't so bad, right? And back in the old times, pirates would berth in tropical islands."

"Wasn't so long ago we were fighting people like that," Robin said in a nostalgic way. "Now we're up against aliens, robots, and an AI. Seriously? What. The. Fuck?"

"You've also gotten a worse mouth on you since this started," Valerie observed.

"Goes with the territory, I guess." Robin shrugged, but a look of worry came over her. "Don't tell my parents, though, when we see them next. Just...you know."

Valerie nodded, wondering if that "when" should be an "if." The chance of Robin seeing her parents again wasn't low, but when and how? They were out here to fight a war whose end they couldn't see. At least, not the larger war's end. This whole thing with the AI, sure; she could see that being over before too long. There wasn't often an enemy who could stand up to her for long, so why should this be any different?

But she had to admit, the month of flying through space had given her time to think, and she missed the feeling of family she'd had around Sandra, Cammie, and the others back home. Robin's presence gave her a different kind of comfort, or had, but since they'd agreed to not share a romantic relationship any more it hadn't been the same. Valerie always felt that when they weren't kicking bad guys' asses, the situation was awkward. Friendly, yes—they were able to converse and have a good time, but in the back of Valerie's mind, especially over the last week, she'd started wondering if she had agreed too easily.

A curious glance from Robin caused Valerie to realize she'd been staring, so she looked back up at the sky.

"What are they, do you think?"

"Those dark shapes?" Robin considered, and as they walked on the haze was parted by a ray of light, but only momentarily. "Ancient gods, frozen in place by the lack of sun this place gets?"

Valerie smiled at her friend. "You and your imagination."

"You have a better idea?"

"Old mountains, carved away by acid rain?" She thought about it, watching one of the shadows. "Maybe massive— Oh *shit!*"

As she spoke one of them moved, lifting into the air and disappearing a moment later, followed by other movements masked by the haze."

"No way did that just happen," Robin said, freezing in her tracks at the same time as Valerie.

"I'm thinking we need to get off this planet as soon as possible."

"Agreed."

"Come on." Valerie took the lead again. This time she was running, trying to keep their bearings but mostly not wanting to come close to those tall shadows in the haze. If something that big attacked her, she wasn't so certain her enhancements would be enough to fight it off. It could be bug-based, more like a massive lizard, or even like a tiger. She had no idea, and didn't want to find out.

They ran through the haze, leaping over ledges and mounds of clay-like earth. In some places old metal rods and tubes stuck out of the ground, as if a scrapyard had been buried here long ago. Their stamina kept them moving; neither worried about running out of breath anytime soon, and they were glad they had left Arlay behind.

"On your left," Robin said, pointing and dodging right.

Valerie followed without bothering to look, but a glance over her shoulder made her glad she had. The haze shifted and a shadow moved through it, and then something that looked like a pillar of obsidian made contact with the ground, scattering clay as it lifted again and came down a second time.

"Holy hell," she said, running sideways before turning to look where she was going. Her foot hit one of the ridges and she sprawled forward, face slamming into the ground.

"Incoming!" Robin shouted, and Valerie lifted her head as the woman scrambled to stop, then ran back and grabbed her. The two rolling aside as another of those massive legs—if that's what they were—came at them.

One more roll and they were clear of it, though the clay showered down on them in red and orange clods. Now they had a better view, and it was clear this wasn't an animal. More...metallic?

Valerie shared a look with Robin and the two were up,

sprinting away as fast as possible. They nearly slammed into a third runner, this one tall and orange—a Lavkin. He was male, judging by the build and harsh features, and turned to them in shock.

"You don't belong here!" he shouted, clutching something to his chest. He looked up at the shadows and squealed, pushing himself faster now. Valerie and Robin were able to overtake him easily, and saw what he was running toward—a cave ahead.

"What the hell *is* that thing?" Valerie asked.

"You're not with them?" the male replied.

"We're with you, if you're part of the closest city."

He looked confused, but just shook his head and said, "As long as you're not trying to kill me, I couldn't give two Alrick's hairs who you are. Follow me."

With that he jumped and slid down a slope, and was up and into the cave a few seconds later. They followed more clumsily since they didn't know the terrain, and as soon as they were in, the male turned back and hit something, shutting them in darkness.

The Lavkin turned to them, likely assuming they couldn't see in the dark, and started to slowly and carefully back away.

"What's he doing?" Robin asked, her tone amused.

"I think he's trying to sneak off," Valerie answered, and the Lavkin froze.

"You can see me?"

Valerie laughed. "Who are you, and what was that out there?"

After a moment, he said, "My name is Osh." He lifted a corner of the package he clasped and placed his hand on what looked like a stone within, which began to glow brightly pink. He stepped forward, assessing the two. "And you?"

"Valerie, and this is Robin. You haven't answered us."

"I'm having a hard time understanding how you got here, and yet have no idea what the Glorock City is."

"A city?" Robin asked. "I'm sorry, but...what?"

"You really aren't from here?" Osh shook his head, looking utterly baffled. "We don't get many visitors, unless..." His eyes went wide. "Oh, you're...you're with *him*."

Valerie's heart skipped a beat and she leaned forward. "Lolack, the leader of the Lost Fleet. You've heard of him?"

"He was here, yes...but no more."

Valerie leaned back, deflated. "But someone might know where he went?"

"Yes, someone might."

"And the Glorock thing?" Robin asked, still glancing back at the doorway occasionally as if it would blast open at any moment.

"Come on. We'll talk on the way." Osh started walking, having to bend slightly in this tunnel. It was the right size for the humans, though. "There are two types of Lavkins here. Mine, the worshipers of Eran, and theirs, those who would live above. The Glorocks."

"And your city...it's where Lolack was last seen, to your knowledge?"

Osh glanced back, licked his lips, and squinted. "You're asking the wrong Lavkin. But yes, my city has the right person to be asking, if that's what you need to know. Just ahead here."

They went through a straight tunnel. It wasn't a short journey, but Osh wouldn't give them any more answers other than that the Glorocks were their enemies, a group that had gone out on their own, refusing to worship the great Eran. He seemed bitter about the whole thing, so Valerie did her best to change the subject.

"This Eran...is he one of you?"

Osh glanced back again, looking even more annoyed now and muttering as he continued walking. Fine, maybe talking about their god was off-limits.

"You're not the most open, are you?" Robin cut in, not even bothering to hide the irritation in her voice."

"Sorry?" He spun on them.

"What, it's part of your culture or something? Two beautiful women show up and this is how you treat them?"

Osh laughed. "Beautiful? This..." He scanned them, then made a disgusted face. "You couldn't be further from beauty, no offense."

"Much offense taken," Robin said, stepping up to him. "The point is that you're being a bit of a dick, while—"

"And you're being a vagina!" He looked utterly confused in addition to being angry, and Valerie couldn't help but laugh.

"Translation issue again," Valerie said, then held a hand up to tell Robin to back off. "Listen, Osh, we got off on the wrong foot. All we're doing is trying to find our friend. If you want us to continue in silence, fine...as long as we get some answers in your city."

The Lavkin took a moment to compose himself, then glanced between Robin and Valerie and sighed. "I under-stand, but look at this from my position, okay? Two crazy-looking aliens show up while I'm running for my life, and for all I know you're with them. I have a family, okay? Ten little ones waiting back there for me, and I could be leading these ugly-as-elivites aliens into our city when they're actually flesh-eating parasites. How do I know you aren't going to try and take them from me and kill us all?"

Valerie blinked, caught off-guard. Everything he had said made sense, in a weird, messed-up way. The number of times she had worried about her loved ones was beyond comprehension so she certainly understood, though in all fairness, she had never had aliens show up on her doorstep.

Vampires and Weres, yes, but not aliens. And those vampires had taken everything from her. A hollow feeling crept into her chest, then expanded into her throat. She had no idea how to answer this Lavkin.

Osh wiped his eyes, and she realized he was crying.

Robin turned to Valerie with a horrified expression, then stepped back in a "You deal with this" way.

"We...we come in peace," she said, quoting one of the movies they'd watched very recently. It felt right, but his teary-eyed look of confusion showed her that it wasn't nearly enough.

"Oosh, we—"

"It's 'Osh.'" He wiped an eye again, then stood up straight; he was trying to be brave, it seemed. "Not 'Oosh.'"

"Yes, I'm sorry. *Osh*." Valerie tried not to let that distract her from what she was about to say, but it took a moment to find the words. "All I can do is tell you the truth, right? We're part of a war out there, and this Lolack character used to lead a great fleet with the power to defeat an evil artificial intelligence that is trying to form an alliance of evil-doers and take over. That's all we're here for—to do our part against this force."

He squinted, still not sure, but slowly nodded. "Go on."

"Go on?" She shook her head, not sure what else there was to say, but then shrugged. "We come from Earth, and we did our part there too. But listen…Robin," she gestured to the woman, "left her mother and father on Earth to come out here and help fight evil, to fight for justice where the weak couldn't defend themselves. And me? I lost what really mattered to me long ago, but recently a friend—a very close friend—gave birth to a beautiful child. I'm not going to be able to see that child grow up because I'm out here fighting for justice too. So... All we can ask is for your trust and cooperation, but please know that we don't mean you or yours harm."

Osh considered this, eyes still narrowed, but they slowly returned to normal. He took a deep breath before saying, "Very well."

And then he turned back around and continued walking. Simple as that.

Valerie and Robin shared a very baffled look, then went after him.

"That's all you have to say?" Robin asked.

Osh smiled at her. "Hey, your friend asked for trust and help, so I'm giving you both. Deep conversation wasn't part of the bargain."

"Are all Lavkins like you?"

"Hardly. Most aren't as tall or attractive as I am. Or as good at stealing Elrocks."

"You stole that?" Valerie asked, figuring he was referring to the glowing rock in his bundle.

He nodded. "Of course. That's how we do it. Without the rocks, we have no way of lighting the city. They steal them on raids and we set up better defenses, then send people like me out to retrieve them. It's incredibly dangerous, and I'm extremely brave."

"Clearly," Robin said with a roll of her eyes.

They cleared the main tunnel and turned left, and soon reached a round door that opened from top to bottom in two halves at a touch from the Lavkin. He gestured them forward, and they went first. After a few stairs, they emerged into a city that, though surrounded by the murky skies, was actually quite clear. A breeze flowed around them, and Valerie imagined the air quality had to do with that.

Massive stone pillars supported a stone ceiling far above, so that the city looked like it was in a large temple. The buildings had stone and metal barricades, and it was clear that a metal wall half the height of the pillars had been pulled back.

"This is home," Osh said, beaming, and then bowed to something on the other side of the city.

Valerie and Robin observed that he was bowing to several large shapes; shadows in the murky sky outside the city.

"More...walking city?" Valerie asked.

"No, no." He straightened from his bow and pointed. "Watch."

As they watched the sky around one of the shadows cleared, and it was revealed to be nothing like the ones they'd encountered before they met Osh. It was a tall image of a Lavkin warrior, staring away from the city with its head bowed. Now that they were paying closer attention, it was clear that these statues were evenly spaced around the city, as evidenced by more shadows, though the far side was dark. Straining her eyes now, Valerie saw that it wasn't darkness, it was rock. The whole city was built right into the side of a mountain. Carved into it, perhaps.

"These are your gods?" Valerie asked cautiously.

Osh chuckled. "Of course not. They represent us to Eran when she shows herself. They keep her from exacting her wrath upon us, so that in their worship of her, she is appeased and might turn away.

So this god was some sort of large being, one who "exacted its wrath" upon the Lavkins at times—or had at some point. She didn't believe in aliens' gods, even if she didn't know what she did believe in, so Valerie found herself wracking her mind for what this so-called god might be. She didn't see any other signs that might be clues as Osh led them into the city.

At an angular building not far from the outskirts of the city, Osh paused to speak with three well-armed Lavkin guards. They glanced at the women more than once, argued, then laughed, then argued some more.

Finally they nodded and walked off.

"What was that?" Valerie asked when they had finished conversing.

"I vouched for you, meaning that you have nothing to worry about. One even offered up one of the city's recently vacated rooms for you two to stay in."

"Stay?" Robin turned to Valerie. "I don't think we're staying, right?"

"Well, you can't leave with what's coming," Osh said with a confused frown. "Oh, right—you don't know how this place works. Well, the guards have promised to get you an audience with the one Lavkin who will have your answers, but not until the storm has passed...and then she might still be asleep."

"So tomorrow," Valerie said, internally groaning.

"Tomorrow. In the meantime, please don't do anything that would make me regret vouching for you. Your story convinced me, and I'd hate to be proven wrong. Come, I'll show you to your room. If you watch closely tonight, you might even catch a glimpse of our god. She likes to come out during the storms."

Valerie nodded, and thanked him for vouching for them. As they followed him to their room, she found herself quite curious. She had never seen a god before. A Dark Messiah, sure, but never a god.

CHAPTER TEN

The observation deck on *Flamebird* was quickly becoming one of Kalan's favorite places, especially in the morning. As someone who'd lived most of his life aboard a spaceship, it was oddly quaint to wake up to the same view every morning, and it helped that it was a beautiful one.

He loved looking out over the water that stretched to the horizon, and the sunrise was a burst of different combinations of vibrant colors every morning. Today the horizon glowed a minty green, with streaks of red shooting out from the rising sun like a lizard bursting forth from its egg.

Kalan enjoyed the silence of the morning and the tranquil serenity of the view before him. He sipped his tea, a pungent and slightly bitter beverage brewed from a particular type of seaweed that grew in the shallows near the island. At first sip he'd almost spat it out, but day by day he was acquiring a taste for the stuff. He'd heard that there was a potent liquor some families made from the same seaweed. He hadn't tried it yet—Lien's family abstained from consuming alcohol—but maybe tonight he would go looking. He imagined that the bitter flavor would taste especially nice with an alcoholic kick.

"Can you believe this is our mission?" Bob asked.

Kalan jerked his head around, surprised to see the human. That was unusual. A childhood spent watching his back in prison had made him very difficult to catch off-guard, so maybe the island lifestyle was making him soft. "I suppose it beats trying to break a political prisoner out of SEDE," Kalan allowed.

"Or fighting a crazy cyborg on a moon of Tol," Bob added.

Kalan couldn't disagree. "Seems like you're adjusting well to life on Rewot. Did I see you chatting with Harlo yesterday?"

Bob grimaced. "Yeah. I don't want to talk about it."

A smile crept onto Kalan's face. "You know, there are few better ways to pique my interest in something than saying, 'I don't want to talk about it.' Now you have to tell me."

Bob sighed. "Fine. I was asking about his sister Dran. You know her?"

Kalan almost choked on his tea. "Wait, you're trying to date a Lavkin girl?"

"I was *trying*," he grumbled. "Turns out it's quite the process. I can't just go on a date with her. Her entire family has to come along, and I'm expected to bring my family along."

"Did you mention that you don't have any family in this star system?"

"I did, to which Harlo replied that I was welcome to

bring you and Jilla instead. He said that since I lived and worked with you, you were basically my family."

"Ha." Kalan had to admit he saw the Lavkin's point. The way they lived, worked, and fought with their families was not that different than the way Valerie lived, worked, and fought with her Elites.

"Totally not worth the effort. It's a shame, though. Dran is pretty hot."

"Did I ever mention you have very strange taste in females?"

Bob cracked a smile. "Yeah. I even liked your mom."

Kalan opened his mouth to tell Bob what he thought of people talking about his mother like that, but before he could something near the horizon caught his eye. For a moment, he thought it was nothing—a handful of specks in an otherwise unmarred morning sky. Maybe a flock of birds, or whatever flying creatures they had here on Rewot. But as he stared at them the specks grew to the size of dots, then became dark shadows on the sky. And they didn't move like any birds Kalan had ever seen.

"Holy shit," Kalan muttered. "It's the Pallicons."

Bob's head snapped in the direction Kalan was looking. He stared in silence for a moment, then said, "My God, you're right. We need to tell somebody."

Kalan nodded slowly, transfixed as he stared at the approaching fighters. He tore his gaze away from them. "Let's find Lien."

They'd only taken a few steps when the alarms began to blare. Kalan and Bob immediately took off, heading for the artillery command center. They'd been assigned to some of the ship's many railguns in the event of an attack.

"I guess we weren't the only ones who got up early," Bob said as they trotted toward their artillery stations.

"You know they have people on watch, right?" Kalan asked. "It wasn't someone who just happened to wake up early and see it."

"Yeah," he answered in an unconvinced tone. "Of course. I'm not stupid."

They met Jilla heading down the long corridor that led to Artillery. "Morning, boys. Ready to blow some of my fellow Pallicons out of the sky?"

"You know it," Kalan said with a grin.

They entered the artillery room, and Lien's nephew Larence, the commander of the ship, pointed them toward their stations.

They squeezed into their seats and grasped the railguns' controls.

"This a super-uncomfortable," Bob muttered as he squirmed in the Lavkin-designed seat. It was both too tall and too narrow for him.

Kalan was struggling to get comfortable as well. The narrow rounded back of the chair didn't accommodate his broad muscular shoulders well. "You're telling me."

"I don't know what you guys are complaining about," Jilla said with a smile as she shifted her form. A moment later she looked like a Lavkin, and fit into the chair fine.

Commander Larence ran over to them and touched each of their controls. Like most Lavkin technology, the railguns needed to be activated by a Lavkin's touch.

His controls active, Kalan gazed intently at the monitor and the now-very-close fighter ships on it. He picked one on the far-left side of the squadron and opened fire. He

PRIME ENFORCER

was surprised to see how quickly the fighter began evasive maneuvers and dodged his fire.

"Let me take the controls," Wearl said in his ear.

"What?" Kalan whispered. "No! I'm doing fine."

"Then ask Larence to give me control of another gun."

Kalan aim and fired again, and this time he was rewarded with a burst of smoke from one of the fighter's engines. A moment later it spiraled toward the ground. "Ha! Pretty good shooting, huh?"

"Kalan," Wearl pleaded, "can't you just—"

"Wearl, now's not exactly the best time to explain I have an invisible companion. Please sit this one out!"

There was a long pause, then Wearl said, "You called me your companion!"

"Don't read too much into it."

More fighters were appearing on Kalan's monitors; they seemed to come from every direction at once. The Lavkin fleet had a brutal capacity for firepower, but against these numbers it was still going to be a fight. Kalan could only imagine how overwhelming it would be when the Wandarby cultists focused on one ship.

Now that he thought of it, he noticed a lot of the Palli-cons' fire was focused on *Flamebird*.

"It's us!" Larence called. "*Flamebird* is their target. Let's get in position!"

Around them, Lavkins stood up and started filing out of the control room.

"Uh, what's this now?" Bob asked, confusion clear in his voice.

"Shit," Larence muttered, frowning when he saw them

still seated. "We didn't cover the protocol for an attack on *Flamebird* with you, did we?"

"Nope," Jilla said.

The commander rubbed the bridge of his nose. "Okay, here's the short version. The Pallicons have recently been attempting to board their target ship after wearing it down a little with a barrage of attacks from the air. In that instance, the target ship is supposed to trust the other ships' gunners to keep the fighters off us and fight off any attackers who manage to board. Just grab a weapon and follow me. We'll find a place for you."

"Wait," Wearl said excitedly. "We get to fight them up close?"

Having given his explanation, the commander hustled out the door after his troops.

Kalan, Bob, and Jilla followed him back to Kalan's favorite place: the observation deck.

"They land a transport on top of us and try to board. If and when that happens, we'll take care of them."

"*Yeah* we will." Kalan drew his trusty Tralen-14. Valerie had given him a whole crate of the things as a gift, because he kept losing his or having it taken away by enemies. He always carried one, and now he was glad he did.

As good as the prospect of defending the ship by fighting the enemy up close and personal sounded, it was frustrating to watch the battle from the observation deck. The ship rocked with each hit from the Wandarby fighters, but so far the hull was intact. When they started taking on water, they'd know they were in trouble.

Kalan glanced at Jilla, and was surprised to see she was still in the shape of a Lavkin.

When he asked her about it, she grinned sheepishly. "I thought it might raise too many questions if they saw one of their own kind fighting for the enemy. I'd rather they don't think too hard about us and why we're here."

"Smart," Kalan said.

Then he saw it through the window behind Jilla: a large transport was headed straight at them, flanked by a dozen fighters who blasted away at the ships, providing cover fire. The transport flew closer, then disappeared from view after it passed the window. A moment later *Flamebird* shook, bobbing in the water as the transport landed on top of them.

"Should we go out there?" Kalan asked.

Commander Larence shook his head. "The fighters would pick us off. They'll try to board, then we'll kick their teeth in."

"I knew I liked you, Commander," Kalan said.

There were fifteen Lavkins on the enclosed observation deck, plus Kalan and his friends. None of them spoke as they waited, having taken cover behind the long metal seats around the room. They'd be semi-protected, but able to shoot at anyone who came through the doors.

They heard a thump as something hit the hatch that led to an airlock. Clearly that was where the Pallicons were trying to get in.

Commander Larence turned to the group. "These beings are attacking your ship. Your home. Your inheritance. Let's smash them into the ground."

A moment later a boom shook the ship and the airlock door flew inward, blown off its hinges by some explosive. Twenty-five Pallicon soldiers burst through the doorway.

Kalan and his friends immediately began firing on the Wandarby cultists. They'd each taken down one before the entire group had made it through the door.

"I'll be back," Wearl shouted in Kalan's ear. "I'm going to see if they have more explosives."

Kalan barely registered the remarks. He was too busy attacking.

A few minutes into the battle, Kalan noticed something strange. The Pallicons were all staring at him in wide-eyed wonder.

Apparently he wasn't the only one to notice their strange behavior.

"I'm an idiot," Commander Larence said loudly. "They know we have a Bandian now! We have to make sure none of them leave here alive."

An explosion much bigger than the one that had blown out the airlock door came from above them, shaking the ship violently.

A moment later Wearl was next to Kalan again, and spoke in his ear. "It turned out they did have more explosives. I used them to blow up their transport."

The Pallicons shouted into their radios even as they tried to fight. Kalan couldn't hear everything they were saying, but he did make out the words "Bandian" and "extraction."

He glanced at the observation window and spotted another approaching transport.

"They've got reinforcements incoming!" he yelled. If he'd understood the snippets of conversation, the Pallicons had called for extraction, and with the reinforcements, Kalan didn't know if they could stop that from happening.

The Pallicons let out a collective cheer as they saw the transport and fell back, exiting through the door they'd blown open.

Kalan started to follow them, but someone grabbed his shoulder.

"You have to stay here," Commander Larence ordered. "We can't risk more Pallicons spotting you." He and the other Lavkins ran after the enemy troops.

"Hey!" Bob shouted to Kalan. "Remember that thing we talked about? With Jilla and Wearl?"

Kalan remembered the plan Bob had suggested: sending Jilla and Wearl to infiltrate the Wandarby cult. He was opening his mouth to say it was still a bad idea, but Jilla spoke first.

"He's right. It's going to be chaos getting their soldiers onto the second transport. We're not going to get a better chance than this."

Kalan considered objecting, but he knew she was right. This was a golden opportunity. "You'll need a uniform. How about that one?" He pointed to a dead Pallicon near them.

"That's a captain's uniform. I want a grunt's so I can stay anonymous. That one!"

Wearl pulled the body she'd indicated over, and Jilla shifted back to her Pallicon form and started changing into the dead soldier's clothes.

A few moments later she was dressed.

"Be careful," Kalan said. "Both of you."

"We're infiltrating an enemy cult," Jilla replied. "I don't think 'careful' is on the menu, but we'll do our best. Come on, Wearl."

She headed for the airlock and the transport beyond.

Kalan and Bob watched through the observation window as the transport flew away. The Pallicon fighters followed.

"Did we win?" Bob asked.

Kalan considered that a moment. The Pallicons had failed to destroy *Flamebird*, but they had learned a Bandian was here with the Lavkin squadron. He didn't yet know if Jilla and Wearl had managed to get aboard the transport, and even if they had, it remained to be seen whether their mission would be successful.

"Honestly, Bob, I'm not sure," Kalan admitted.

CHAPTER ELEVEN

Osh had left Valerie and Robin at a strange mud hut with sleeping mats of vibrant green, which were way too long for them. Before they could get situated, the doors slid open and a thin female Lavkin appeared, eyes wide at the sight of them. She looked very much like Osh, but her skin was adorned with red paint in swirling patterns and she had gold leaves plastered to her forehead.

"You two speak our language?" the female asked.

"No, but we have translators," Valerie replied, then wondered if it would've just been easier to say yes. To her relief, the female nodded.

"My name is Swarne," the female said as she stepped in. After a quick glance around, she frowned. "My apologies that we couldn't get you better accommodations. My brother tells me you're here for word of that strange Lolack?"

Valerie nodded. "Do you know anything about him?"

"Only that he was here, and that he spoke mostly with

the one you're meeting tomorrow. I was sent by her to ensure you have everything you need."

"And maybe to see if we're trustworthy? Safe?"

"Not at all. If Osh says you're safe, we are good with that. You see, Osh has the ability to judge someone's character. He's never been wrong."

"Is that so?" Valerie smirked, doubting it.

"He said you both have sordid pasts and you have taken lives, but that it is not your intent to do so here." Now it was Swarne's turn to smile, and she cocked her head. "Is that correct?"

Valerie shifted on her feet uneasily. "He guessed all that from speaking with us for a few minutes?"

"As I said, very in tune with the universe, my brother. The rest, less so." Her eyes moved from one to the other; she seemed to be overwhelmed. "My apologies! It's just that we don't see too many visitors, and we've never seen your type. What do they call you?"

"'Humans,'" Robin replied. "And sometimes 'badass chicks.'"

"Let's stick with humans," Valerie said with a laugh, then nudged Robin.

"And the planet you are from…it's different from ours?" Swarne asked. "More...beautiful?"

"It was, once," Robin said.

"There are parts that still are." Valerie remembered her time in the fjords of Norway, with their rolling green hills and water glimmering in the sunset. There was no doubt that many parts of Earth were still incredible, but Robin had a limited view of the world. It made sense, considering her more recent transformation to a vampire. That took time to get over, and the craving for human blood was certain to change your outlook on life.

She was glad neither of them had that craving anymore.

"You know," Robin began, taking a minute to look at the ground, then at her hands. She seemed to be analyzing them. "She's right. It's not all bad, but it's really the people who make it what it is. Like here... I saw your brother's love for his family. That! That right there is what I see as the true beauty of any world."

"Your family, it is big like ours?" Swarne asked.

Robin shook her head, looking wistful. "No, it's just my parents and me. They wanted more, but they're growing old. Too old for that, honestly. Always wanted a sister and they always wanted to give me one, but..."

"Earth has had its problems," Valerie interjected. "Even if a couple *can* have children, the situation doesn't always allow it. Or didn't, anyway. We worked to change that, and I think we did a damn good job."

"Otherwise we would still be there fighting for a better world," Robin said, her sorrow giving way to a smile. She looked at Valerie and held her gaze.

After a moment, Swarne cleared her throat. "I will be there tomorrow. If you would be so kind, I would love to hear more about it, but now I will let you get your sleep."

"Thank you," Valerie said, and Robin repeated it as the female departed.

The hut was better than sleeping on the ship, but their comms didn't work here, so they worried that the others would start to wonder about them. Gentle music was playing, as soft and melodic as if it were one with the cool breeze blowing through the open window. Valerie went to it, staring out at the vast carvings of worshiping Lavkins looming over the land as the coming storm and murky sky blocked out the stars.

Kalan was out there somewhere. She hoped he and the others were safe, but knew he could handle himself.

How could places like this exist in the universe, and so many people—races of aliens, even—not know? They would never witness its beauty or its perfection, yet here she was with Robin. A glance back at the young woman, who was curled up on the mat with her eyes on the statues as well, and Valerie started to think maybe they could stay here as long as they wanted. It was so peaceful, so beautiful. There was no question in her mind what had brought Lolack here.

And staring at Robin, she wondered if the woman was lying there like that on purpose. Like maybe she wanted Valerie to come to her, to embrace her and lie with her. Maybe?

She cocked her head and Robin's eyes moved to hers. There was a gentle smile on her lips. Those perfect lips.

Valerie removed her body armor and laid down behind Robin, wrapping an arm around her.

"Um, what the fuck?" Robin asked, body instantly going rigid.

Valerie pulled her hand back, sitting up as if shocked. "Oh shit. Read that wrong?"

"I'm lying here relaxed, ready to get some well-earned sleep...and you take that as a sign to what...cop a feel?"

"I didn't cop anything!"

"There was definite side-boob grazing." Robin sat up now too, on the other side of the mat. She put her face in her hands and Valerie wondered if she were crying, but then heard her laugh.

"This is funny?"

Robin stood, arms spread wide. "Yes, actually. In that ironic way, not the ha-ha way. Come on, Val! Is this place amazing? Of course, but that doesn't mean we should revert to our old ways, or that the war out there is any less pressing."

With that, Robin went to the corner where her armor was and began dressing.

"Where are you going?" Valerie demanded.

"I need some fresh air."

"You mean you need a break from me?"

"No," Robin fastened her chest plate. "It's you who needs a break from me."

"Don't be like that," Valerie said. She went to the door after her, but Robin was walking faster than Valerie cared to. Dammit, she'd made a mistake...she saw that.

It was the perfection of this place; like a drug that promised its user everlasting bliss, but apparently had its side effects. She wanted to hit herself, then run after Robin and apologize. Promise to never even look at her like that again.

Instead, she laid back on the mat and covered her face with a pillow, then screamed into it. Although she had come to realize life out here was about the bigger picture, and although she had told herself that she was bigger than love and relationships, she was still a woman in her mid-thirties, depending on how one judged age for a vampire. She chose to go with the version that put her in her mid-thirties. To give up on emotions and feelings at that age was a strength even she didn't possess.

She let the pillow fall to the side of the mat and lay staring at the ceiling for several minutes. If she were on Earth, what would she do? Likely go find her friend Sandra and ask *her* what to do, she realized with a laugh. Sandra would say you could do it all; that ignoring one's needs and feelings would, in the end, lead to more distractions than following through with them in the first place.

Well, damn. Robin certainly wasn't there. Maybe that meant Valerie would have to fight for her, or... Or respect her feelings and be open to other avenues of love.

Damn, this was all so complicated. She'd much rather run into the street, find a bad guy, and kick his or her ass.

How was it, she wondered, that she had become this person? A superpowered vampire—if she could even call herself that anymore—who felt more comfortable with violence that emotions? If her parents were still alive, she couldn't believe they'd look too highly on that.

The music continued to drift in, but it started to feel less peaceful and more melancholy; perhaps even creepy. Each note seemed to pluck at Valerie's bones, sending a chill through her and reminding her that Robin had gone out alone on an alien planet.

Sure it was peaceful and beautiful; almost perfect, even. But it was plain sense that you didn't split up in situations like this. While she hadn't seen many movies during her time with Bad Company, she did know enough to understand that this was not a good thing.

Now she understood it—the fascination with films. They weren't just fun, they were educational. Like that one about a mermaid that she had watched at least three times before taking off on their mission, which had taught her that it was smart to do what you think is best, even if your parents disagreed. In the end, she had gotten her legs and her man after all. Valerie was determined to watch more movies when she had a chance to see what other values humans had once had, when they'd had time and energy to produce those majestic creations.

With a sigh she stood and threw her armor back on, intent on finding Robin to make sure she was okay. Nothing more, though. She hoped they wouldn't run into trouble, wandering the city without an escort.

CHAPTER TWELVE

The Pallicon transport was crowded with smelly battle-soiled soldiers, each of whom were dealing with the lack of space in their own way. Some shifted to a thin form not unlike that of the Lavkins. A few tried to assert their dominance by shifting to a larger-than-normal shape in order to take up even more room. The majority suffered in silence, enduring the crowded space with sour looks on their faces, but without complaining loud enough for their superior officers to hear them.

Jilla tried to blend into that last group. She wanted to attract as little attention as possible. Attention would lead to questions and questions would almost certainly lead to her being found out, so she stayed as still as possible, hoping no one would notice she was out of place.

Wearl, on the other hand, was anything but silent. "Sons of prison troughs! If I get another elbow to the face, I'm going to rip out someone's spine and use it as dental floss."

"Gross," Jilla whispered. She couldn't much blame her friend for her prickly attitude. Being invisible in a crowded space was a surefire way to get trampled feet, and a lot worse. It was crowded enough in the transport that wherever she stood, someone mistook it for an empty place and tried to claim it. Thankfully it was also crowded enough that no one seemed to notice they were bumping against an invisible person.

Eventually, Jilla moved a bit out from the wall and Wearl squeezed in behind her.

The ride up to the Wandarby cult's warship only took twenty minutes, but they were some of the longest of Jilla's life. She half-expected to be found out at any moment. Most of the tough situations in her life she'd been able to fight her way out of. Granted, she had spent a good chunk of time in a Skulla temple, but other than that she'd been pretty lucky. If this went wrong, her luck would end for good. There'd be no chance of talking or fighting her way out of this one.

As their transport ship docked, attaching to an airlock on the large warship, she felt the soldiers collectively exhale. The tension seemed to drain out of them. They were done with their battle, and back home. Many of them began to chatter to each other, giving Jilla the cover she needed to speak to Wearl.

She turned her head and whispered, "Ready?"

"You know I am," Wearl said. "To recap, the plan is for me to access the ship's records, get all the intel I can, and then get us out of here?"

"Yes," Jilla whispered.

"Why'd I bring you along again? It kinda feels like I'm doing the heavy lifting."

"I'll be learning what I can about the cult," Jilla reminded her.

The door to the transport opened and a captain stepped through.

"That's my cue," Wearl announced. "See you when I'm done."

"Good luck," Jilla said, but the lack of answer made her think the Shimmer was already gone.

The captain stood at attention in front of the gathered troops. "The fighting is done. Now is the time for celebration."

A cheer went up among the soldiers.

Jilla had to admit she was getting a better deal than Wearl. A celebration sounded pretty good.

The soldiers marched out of the transport and down a long corridor in the warship. Jilla wedged herself somewhere near the middle so she didn't have to know where she was going, and where she wasn't likely to be spotted by the officer trailing behind them.

The troops eventually made their way through a large set of double doors at the end of the corridor and entered a large, open room lined with benches. Jilla followed the others' lead and took a seat.

The room fell silent as a Pallicon in a simple black robe stepped to the front. He held a single white flower.

"What is this flower?" he asked, holding it aloft.

The troops responded in unison. "It is the universe, the great design, and all good things."

"What am I?" the strange priest asked.

"You are the Bandian," the soldiers intoned. "The Grayhewn. The scourge of the galaxy. The drinker of blood. The killer of children."

"That is correct. And I have returned!" The priest shifted, changing shape from that of a Pallicon to the large, muscular shape of a Bandian. Then he crushed the flower in his hand.

The object lesson over, he immediately transformed back to his true shape.

Then he started talking. And boy, did he talk. On and on, for nearly thirty minutes. He said they now had eyewitness accounts that the Lavkins were harboring at least one Bandian, something the Wandarby had suspected for a longtime.

He told tales of the evils supposedly committed by the ancient Bandians. He told them how they and their evil-worshiping allies the Lavkins were once again on the rise. About how the Wandarby were the faithful few Pallicons dedicated to good. He mentioned something about how the gathered faithful would be united with their fellow believers very soon, but Jilla was barely paying attention at that point.

Just when she thought she couldn't take anymore, she felt a tap on her arm.

"Let's go!" Wearl said. "I got the info and our ride back to Rewot, but we have go now."

Jilla stood up and tried to slide down the aisle without attracting attention. But the moment she stepped into the aisle, the priest stopped speaking and glared at her.

"Where are you going, soldier?" he hissed.

She stood frozen for a long moment, unable to convince her mind to spew out any kind of an answer.

"Say something!" Wearl demanded.

She spoke the first word that came to mind. "Bathroom."

The priest squinted at her as if trying to tell if she was being serious, then nodded and returned to his speech on the evils of gray skin.

When they reached the corridor Wearl said, "Go to the end of the hall and turn right. I found the flight manifests for today. Fighter 7584 is scheduled to head out on a patrol mission in ten minutes. I have all the codes we need, so we can fly that fighter back down to Rewot."

"Okay, but won't the real pilot have something to say about that?"

"I don't think we have to worry about her showing up," Wearl said evenly.

Jilla started to ask what had happened to pilot, but stopped herself. She decided she'd rather not know. "You get anything good?"

Wearl let out an eerie, lilting laugh. "Did I ever! I found this workstation where the guy kept his password written down next to his computer. You know what his password was? Go ahead and guess."

"I really have no—"

"It was 'butts.' His passwords was butts. Do you know how stupid you must be, to not only make that your password but also to write it down because you can't remember it? That's a seriously dumb creature."

"That's great, Wearl, but the info? Did you find anything interesting?"

"I found a whole treasure trove of interesting, and none of it's good. We need to get back to Kalan."

Kalan picked up the broom and started sweeping. It felt like such a small thing. Such an unimportant task, and yet it had to be done. He believed that if you had an idle moment and there was work to be done you might as well do it, even if it wasn't technically your job.

They were still cleaning up the *Flamebird* after the Wandarby cult's attack. The ship had gotten away with relatively little damage, thanks to the squadron's good planning and their quick response. A few doors had been blown off their hinges and there were plenty of dings and scorch marks on the hull, but the ship remained intact. The Pallicon attack had been unsuccessful.

But that didn't mean it had been without cost. Two Lavkins had died during the fighting.

Kalan was trying to occupy his troubled mind with the task at hand, but it wasn't helping. He'd observed the truth firsthand. Although the Lavkins' ships were technological marvels and their weapons were cutting-edge, the orange-skinned creatures weren't the best at fighting up close.

It was no wonder the Pallicons had tried to board. If it hadn't been for Kalan and his friends, the attempt might have been successful. Ultimately the Lavkins had driven the Wandarby cultists off the ship, but by that point they had wanted to leave.

Suddenly, the alarms began blaring again. Kalan's hand immediately went to his Tralen-14, and his eyes went to the big window. A single Pallicon fighter was approaching. He stared at it for a long moment. Why would they send a single fighter?

Then a realization hit him, and he sprinted toward the control room.

When he got there, most of the gunnery stations were already occupied.

"We'll wait until it gets in range," Commander Larence told them, "and then blow it out of the sky."

"Wait!" Kalan shouted.

Every head in the room turned toward him.

"Don't shoot. I think that may be Jilla!"

The commander stared at him blankly. "What makes you say that?"

"Think about it! Why would they send a single fighter to attack us?"

"Could be a suicide mission," one of the gunners suggested.

The commander frowned. "Seems unlikely. They've never used that tactic before. Let's see if we can hail that fighter."

A moment later, Jilla's voice filled the room. "Thank you for not shooting me down. I couldn't figure out this damn radio until you hailed me."

"Good to hear your voice," the commander said. "You can land on the island."

"Got it, thanks. I'll talk to you soon. I have news to share, and it's not the good kind."

CHAPTER THIRTEEN

Wandering through the night, Valerie felt odd at the freedom they had given her. She appreciated it, and could tell the other Lavkins had been briefed on their presence by the way they looked at her, but it was still strange to not be challenged, or at least escorted. She wondered where Robin had gotten to, but she had been strolling around long enough to realize Robin didn't want to be found. Valerie was certain the woman could handle herself if she got in trouble, and she figured a little alone time wouldn't hurt anyone.

Glow stones lined the streets here, and outside the city the storm was coming. Strong winds blew and the night sky flowed with dirt and clods of clay...and then she froze, staring at the massive shadow that moved. Not one of those statues, not the moving city from earlier, but a shape wide and tubular, flailing about and then leaping into the sky and arcing down, taking its time to hit the ground again and plunge in, and then it was gone.

That was their Eran, she realized with a shock. A

massive sand snake, was her best guess. How terrifying that it had been out there, moving about under the ground while they were coming here. She didn't care how strong she was, how much she could heal—if she got eaten by a sand snake, she was pretty sure it would be the end of her.

Or what if she were ground up, but still live? Would she be stuck between constant rejuvenation and being torn apart, feeling eternal pain? There wasn't much that would be more horrific to her mind, so she turned from the storm, arms wrapped around herself against the chill riding up her spine, and made for the center of the city. She wouldn't be able to sleep now and figured it would be fine to go there, since nobody had told her not to.

On the way Valerie tried calling the ship, but only got static. She realized that they might be caught up in the storm, but the ship could handle it. She pushed the thought away, hoping she was right. They would go back tomorrow after the storm was over—and after they had the information they needed—and then be on their way. In the meantime, she had to have faith in them.

In the center of town was a small garden with pools of liquid that she at first thought was water, but when she drew closer she saw that it wasn't reflecting the buildings. It was red. Not blood—she could tell by the smell—but still odd.

A younger-looking Lavkin, teenaged maybe, poked his head out of second-story window.

"You! Crazy lady! Didn't you hear there's a storm coming?"

She smiled up at him and nodded. "I'll be heading back then."

He drew his head back inside and a moment later waved her in. "My parents said for you to join us. We're eating supper still, and have plenty."

Valerie hadn't been expecting it, but when was she going to have an opportunity like this again? She tried to refuse out of politeness, but when he ran downstairs and appeared at the door with his mother, she couldn't say no.

It was surreal, sitting here with this family. There were six children, eating some sort of orange bread and goop on the side that reminded her of extremely spicy mashed potatoes. Mostly it was the feeling of being part of all this, of seeing how families lived on these other planets, that got to her.

Lately she had been in need of a good reminder that these were real planets with real people, not simply allies and enemies in this war she'd found herself a part of. Life wasn't about fighting all the time—at least not for these Lavkins, nor for so many others out there.

And she wanted to keep it that way. These children didn't need to experience that. It was a nice reminder of what she'd left behind. People on Earth and on planets like this—people of all races—deserved to live their lives without being scared.

She fought for *them*.

The storm had died down outside and they told her they were in the calm few minutes before it got really bad, so she had better hurry. They gave her some more bread and she thanked them profusely, then darted into the night to find her hut.

She returned to find Robin deeply asleep and smiled,

feeling bad for again putting her friend in an awkward position with her feelings.

No more.

She left the bread on a portion of the wall that stuck out like a table, then removed her armor and laid down to get some sleep. Even with the whistling winds of the storm and images of that sand snake running through her mind, she managed to pass out after a few minutes.

Life was exhausting sometimes, and wonderful others. Dreams came to her of a grand return to Earth, Robin and Kalan and all the others there with her, walking into a dining hall and being served those amazing steaks Colonel Walton had fed them once upon a time.

Maybe that day was only in her dreams, but it could all come true. They were going to set this universe straight, then enjoy the fruits of their labor—or the steaks of it.

CHAPTER FOURTEEN

"They know we have a Bandian," Jilla told them, "and they are coming to kill him."

The Lavkin leaders listened in silence, their eyes wide with concern. Mej and Lien sat together on a wide chair. Commander Larence and the other ships' commanders were there, too.

"They've been harassing you for the past few months in the hope that they'd provoke you into an attack," she continued. "They were hoping your Bandian allies would reveal themselves, and then they would bring their entire fleet down on your heads."

"And now they know we *do* have a Bandian," Mej said with a sigh.

Jilla nodded. "Of course, they believe we have more than one. They think Kalan showing himself was a mistake, and the rest of them are hiding in the ships. But now that they have a confirmed sighting, they've put out the call to the rest of the fleet—a dozen ships, each as big as the one from which they've been launching attacks."

Lien made a guttural sound that either wasn't a word or one Kalan's translation chip was unable to interpret. "A dozen ships? Each probably has a squadron of fighters."

"We've had a hard enough time fighting off one squadron," Commander Larence added.

A ball of hot guilt burned in Kalan's belly. A fleet was coming here to kill these people, and it was all because of him. "There's only one thing we can do. I need to leave. We have the fighter Jilla stole from the Pallicons. I can fly away from here, and hail them on my way out. They'll chase me and leave you alone."

Mej shook her head. "As noble as that sounds, I don't think it's going to be that easy. As Jilla said, they believe we are hiding other Bandians. Now that they've seen you, it will be incredibly difficult to convince them otherwise."

"What if I surrender myself to them?" Kalan asked. "Maybe even let them search the ships to confirm—"

"You're not getting it," Lien interrupted. "They are a cult. They believe your kind are trying to destroy the fabric of the universe, and that my kind are trying to help. There's no reasoning with these creatures."

"He's right," Jilla said. "I had to sit through one of their little revival meetings. You should have heard the priest! Reality and the Wandarby cultists are not on speaking terms."

The ball of guilt in his stomach was threatening to overwhelm him with its white heat. "So what do we do?"

"I think it's pretty obvious," Bob said, speaking for the first time during the meeting. "We have to fight them."

"Shut up, Bob," Kalan said. "We can't just—"

"No, Kalan, this time I won't shut up. You need to admit it. There's no easy way out here, no tricky plan. It's going to come down to muscle, bullets, and blood."

A wide smile broke across Jilla's face. "As much as I hate to admit it, Bob's right on this one."

Mej nodded. "Jilla says the fleet will be here in the next day or so. There's no allied force that could reach us in time. Converting our ships back to a flyable state would take weeks. Even Valerie couldn't get back here in time if she went where I think she did. We're on our own. We have to defend our homes."

Kalan said nothing. In his heart he doubted their ability to fight off a dozen warships and dozens of fighters, but he'd stand by their sides while they tried. He'd give it everything he had.

Jilla looked up suddenly. "That reminds me, I have something Valerie needs to know, too."

"If Commander Larence will let us use the comm equipment, we can send a message to the *Grandeur*," Bob said.

"Of course," Commander Larence said. "I have a favor to ask as well." He turned to Kalan. "I was wondering if you might work with our people a little bit. I know we don't have time for a lot of training, but the ferocity you and your friends fought with...I've never seen anything like it. If you could give us any tips, we'd certainly appreciate it."

"Of course," Kalan replied. "We'll use every moment of the time we have from now until the attack to prepare."

Mej and Lien exchanged a glance.

"Actually, there is one other thing we need to do

tonight," Mej told them. "If you three are going to fight by our sides, we need to make you part of our squadron. And that means making you part of a family. Lien and I would be honored if you would officially join ours."

Kalan felt a lump rising in his throat. He'd brought these beings nothing but trouble. His very presence had directly led to what would probably be their destruction, and now they wanted to make him part of their family?

"Specifically, we'd like you to join my branch of the family," Lien said. "That means you'll be officially stationed on *Flamebird*. It would be your ship as much as it is mine. You'd have the same rights as any other member of our family."

"We'd be honored," Kalan said, his voice catching a little. "How could we say no?"

"Good, then it's all—"

"Wait," Kalan said, suddenly remembering something. "Before you make us a part of your family, there's something you should know. We haven't been entirely honest with you. There aren't three of us here with you. There are four." He had no idea how they'd react to this announcement. They might be angry that he'd kept Wearl hidden, but they needed to know the truth before they made him part of the family.

The Lavkin looked entirely confused by that statement.

"Have you heard of the Shimmers?" he asked.

Lien scratched his chin. "Yes. Warrior race. Invisible to most biological eyes. Their voices are inaudible to us too, I think. I've heard of them. Never met one, of course."

"Actually, you have. There's been one among you since we arrived. I'd like to introduce you to our friend Wearl."

The Lavkins sat in surprised silence.

"What, am I supposed to give a speech or something?" Wearl asked. "It's not like they could hear me anyway."

"Wearl says she's honored to meet you," Kalan told them.

Commander Larence looked around the room as if he'd see her. "So the Shimmer is here in this room with us?"

Kalan nodded. "She fought in the battle on *Flamebird*. She was the one who blew up the Pallicon transport, and she went with Jilla to the Wandarby warship. In fact, she was the one who got the information from their records."

After a long moment, Mej rose to her feet. "Well, I guess we'll be welcoming four new beings into the family instead of three."

They met on the island that evening. Kalan expected to be the entire squadron again, but it wasn't. There were only Lien, Mej, Commander Larence, and the crew from *Flamebird*—about thirty beings in total. The family into which they were being adopted.

They stood in a circle, with torches set in a ring behind them.

Lien stepped forward after they'd joined the circle. "Tonight's ceremony is quite simple. As members of a family, you are expected to live and be willing to die to protect your new brothers and sisters. Do you have any questions before we begin?"

Bob sheepishly raised a hand. "Uh, this is very nice and

all, but we're not agreeing to like, live on *Flamebird* for the rest of our lives, are we?"

Mej laughed. "Of course not. A family does not hold each other hostage. You are free to leave, always knowing you have a home here with us if you want it."

"Good, because I honestly think Valerie would kick all our asses if we told her we quit the Elites to live on the beaches on Rewot."

Kalan had to admit he was probably right.

Lien continued, "You've been invited to join this family and receive all the rights of any Lavkin. We ask but one thing: as a show of unity with your new family, we ask that you tell us something true."

"Uh, what?" Jilla asked. "Something true? Like water is wet?"

"If you wish," Lien answered with a thin smile. "It's customary to make it something personal. Perhaps even something you wouldn't want shared beyond the family, but the choice is yours as long as it's true."

"It's a sacred rite in our culture," Commander Larence explained. "Weddings, coming-of-age celebrations, important birthdays...telling something true is a way to show your respect for and trust in those gathered."

Kalan looked to the left and saw Jilla looking at him expectantly. He looked to the right and saw Bob giving him the same expression. "All right. Guess I'm first, then."

He thought for a long moment, his mind searching for something true he could reveal that might be worthy of this honor. Everything he thought of seemed inadequate. He could tell them about his father's mission, but that wasn't exactly a secret. He could tell a story from his childhood, but he couldn't think of anything that felt important enough.

Then he thought of it. The one thing he was truly ashamed of in his life. The moment it entered his mind, he knew that was the story he needed to tell. He swallowed hard and took a step forward.

"I grew up in this prison ship called SEDE. Not sure if you've heard of it, but it doesn't matter. Kids born there stay until they turn eighteen. The day before my eighteenth birthday, my mother took me aside. She told me she didn't care what I did when I got out, as long as it made me happy. She told me to follow my dreams and all that, but there was one thing she made me promise. She asked me to swear to her that I would never break the law."

He looked around. They were all watching him, listening intently to his story.

"See, when a kid leaves SEDE, he doesn't have a lot of choices," he continued. "A lot of kids like me fall back on their network of connections, the people they were in prison with. They may not be able to get a straight job, but their SEDE connections can help them start a few rungs up the ladder in the criminal underworld. My mom wanted to make sure I didn't go down that path, and I promised her I wouldn't.

"For the first month after I got out, I got by on the little bit of money my mother had socked away for me in prison. It had seemed like a fortune in SEDE, but in the outside world it didn't go far. I quickly learned that legitimate employers weren't too interested in hiring a kid fresh out of prison, and I started getting hungry. Then I bumped into a guy I'd known inside. He was setting up a crew to steal a shipment of this valuable metal alloy, and he needed some muscle. I took the job."

Kalan looked around, wondering if they would see him differently, but their faces were unreadable.

"The job went off without a hitch, but I felt sick to my stomach the entire time. He offered me another job, and I turned it down. I told him that was the one and only time, and it was. I never stole anything again."

"Except for that Nim fighter from SEDE," Wearl said.

"And the Tralen-14 you took from the Pallicon who tried to highjack that transport you were on," Bob added.

"Fine, I never stole anything that wasn't part of a mission for Valerie, but it didn't really matter. I'd already broken my word to my mother." He stepped back into the ring. "That's it. That's my story."

Lien nodded. "Thank you for sharing that. Welcome to the family."

"Ooh, me next," Wearl said. "Will you repeat my story for them, Kalan?"

"Sure." He listened, then turned to the Lavkins. "Wearl says she once punched a guy so hard one of his teeth got stuck in her knuckle."

Lien's mouth twisted in disgust, but he nodded politely. "It's okay, Wearl. We've all done things we regret."

Wearl said to Kalan, "Oh, I misunderstood. I thought we were telling stories we're proud of."

"Welcome to the family, Wearl," Lien said.

Bob took a step forward. "Okay, my turn. It all started when I was nine." He went on to tell a long, winding story of his first job, his sexual awakening, and his love of a food called 'burritos.' It was a story that seemed to have no point, and no ending. Kalan had to resist the urge to tell him to shut up multiple times. Finally he wrapped up with, "And that's the last time I ever paid for beer and diapers at the same establishment. Phew, it feels good to get that off my chest."

Lien looked a little confused, but he once again nodded. "Very nice, Bob. Welcome to the family."

All eyes turned to Jilla. She took a step forward and drew a deep breath before speaking. "Okay, here goes. Sometimes—not often, mind you, and certainly not right now—I find myself sort of attracted to Bob."

An awkward silence fell over the circle. Bob's jaw had fallen open so wide the Wandarby cultists probably could have flown one of their fighters in there. Kalan fought an almost irresistible urge to laugh.

"Thank you, Jilla," Lien said. "I'm sure that was difficult to admit."

"You don't know the half of it," Jilla replied.

"Welcome to the family."

They spent the next hour mingling and chatting with their new family. Everyone was so warm and welcoming. Kalan was starting to get that this "you'll be part of the family" thing wasn't just words. They took it seriously. Everyone gathered here regarded Kalan, Bob, Jilla, and Wearl as their brothers and sisters.

Kalan wished there was something he could do to repay their kindness. Then he suddenly realized there *was* something he could do.

He tapped Commander Larence on the shoulder. "Excuse me, Commander, do you think you could show me to the comm equipment? I need to get a message to someone as quickly as possible."

Larence looked a little surprised, but he immediately agreed, and the two of them slipped away to send the message.

CHAPTER FIFTEEN

Valerie woke to find Swarne and Osh staring at her with puzzled looks on their faces.

"Why do you roar when you sleep?" Osh asked.

"Are you angry?"

"What?" Valerie sat up and stretched, then adjusted her shirt because she realized it was revealing her chest.

"Ah, gross," Osh said, glancing away. "Sorry, I mean..."

Valerie frowned and stood. Robin was sitting cross-legged, grinning at her. "What? What are you all talking about?"

"Snoring," Robin explained, then turned to their guests. "Some humans do that. It's weird, huh?"

They both nodded in agreement.

"Wait, hold on!" Valerie rotated her neck, ignoring the cracking. "There's no way I snore."

Robin shrugged, and the other two insisted she had been snoring.

"Agh, whatever." She glanced around, remembering

where she was, and realized there was no separate bathing room. "I don't suppose you have showers? Baths?"

"Didn't you go by the bathing pool last night?" Swarne asked. "Come. I can show you, but I think you know the way."

Valerie glared. "You mean...the red pool in the middle of town?"

"Yes, you do know it!"

"I'm...not going to bathe in front of a bunch of you, where everyone's eyes can wander."

Robin laughed. "No? You're super-shy all of a sudden?"

"I just don't want to be nude in a place where every man looks at me with disgust," Valerie countered. "That's ass-backwards, first of all, because," she turned to Osh and glared, "I'm hot as hell."

"Hot as hell?" Osh laughed, and couldn't stop.

Valerie didn't want to ask if it was about the statement, which maybe he had never heard before, or if it was at her insistence that she was hot.

"Brother, that's rude," Swarne said, grabbing his nose. He instantly stopped. "Surely they know they're hideous, and don't need to be reminded of it."

"Wait, don't bring me into this," Robin protested.

Everyone stood in awkward silence for a moment while Valerie pulled her hair back and put on her armor. She said, "Shall we get on with it?"

"Yes!" Swarne smiled, glad someone had broken the silence. "Wokana looks forward to meeting you. We've told her so many great things."

"You hardly know us."

"We know enough," Osh said, then leaned toward her

and said in a very friendly way, "And don't worry, we didn't say anything about your looks."

"For the love of…" Valerie walked past him, then stopped and looked back, glaring. Her lip starting to pull up at the corner. "*You!*"

She wanted to run back and hit him, because he had started cracking up, slapping his sister on the shoulder and pointing.

"Sorry," Swarne said with a shrug. "He likes to mess with strangers."

"So you *don't* think we're hideous?" Robin asked as she joined Valerie.

"Not my type at all," Osh said, trying to calm his laughter. "But come on, I'm not an idiot, and I'm not blind."

Valerie shook her head. "Maybe I'm looking forward to leaving this planet after all," she said to Robin.

Robin nodded, not making eye contact. Great, she was still annoyed about the previous night. Valerie made a mental note to come back to that when they weren't on their way to meet an alien leader.

"Only asking to be certain," Osh asked from behind. "The bath…did you want to?"

"No, I'll pass," Valerie replied, not bothering to hide the irritation in her voice.

The Lavkin siblings led them to their destination, though Valerie was pretty certain Osh was let down about her not taking a bath. She had a feeling he was playing down his attraction to her, or was at least curious.

They stopped at a home not so different from the rest, except for being taller and having a pointed top. Swarne gestured for them to wait outside with Osh, then stepped inside. A moment later she reappeared and said, "You may enter."

The inside was—surprisingly—not so different from the hut they had slept in, though it had more rooms and carvings in the walls. Some of the carvings related to great battles, and at one spot there were the guardian statues and the image of a sand snake.

"Did you see her?" Osh asked, as they waited for their host.

Valerie nodded, but noticed Robin frowning. Trying to clue her in, she added, "Your god is a sight to behold indeed."

"She can be full of wrath, but she is our god."

Robin glanced between Valerie and the image of the snake, then tried to do her best to hide the disgust on her face. A giant sand snake wasn't Valerie's idea of the best deity either, but she wasn't going to insult others' religions.

Wanting to say something before the conversation went there, she turned and admired the images on the far wall. They showed two groups of people standing and facing each other, and between them was a holder for a glowing stone. It had a cracked stone in it, which was not glowing.

"And the meaning of that?" Valerie asked.

Swarne approached it and touched the stone. For a moment it glowed, but then the glow faded.

"You see," she explained, "the cracked stone can't hold a charge, just like a family separated can't continue on forever."

"There's way too much about what you just did and said that didn't make sense," Valerie said. "First of all..." She walked over and touched the stone. Nothing. "How'd you do that? I saw Osh do the same yesterday."

"It's what we do," Swarne replied.

Robin shrugged. "Maybe Lavkins are more conductive than humans?"

"I…" Valerie shook her head, realizing she wasn't going to understand it. "Okay, and the family? You mean the others on the moving city?"

Swarne nodded, but looked hesitant to talk. Her eyes flitted to the side room, where a female Lavkin stood. They had a similar look, but this one appeared older and wore flowing red robes.

"May I present our leader Wokana, High Priestess of Eran." Osh bowed his head and stepped aside.

The high priestess entered and Valerie and Robin both bowed as Osh had, but just with their heads.

"To answer your question," Wokana said, "they turned their backs on Eran. The other half of our family, there." She gestured to the carving on the wall. "We have been at each other's throats over the stones ever since."

"I'm sorry to hear it," Valerie replied.

"But we haven't met here to talk about our problems, have we?" Wokana asked. "To what do we owe this visit?"

"There was a certain traveler who came through here at one point. Lolack was his name. Admiral Lolack."

Wokana's eyes lit up at that, but she took a moment to answer. "Perhaps our story and yours have more interconnection than I realized." She motioned for Osh and Swarne to come close, then lowered her voice as she added, "This doesn't leave the room."

They nodded, looking very intrigued.

"You see," Wokana said, turning back to her guests, "we're by law and religion not permitted to ask outsiders for help in this matter, but your mission to find Admiral Lolack directly affects us. You can find him while achieving what we would ask of you."

"Which is?"

"We have one source of food, and it is cultivated with the use of the stones."

Valerie clenched her jaw, not liking where this was going. "So you want us to get them back?"

Wokana considered her, then shook her head. "Not exactly. Admiral Lolack was here, but he went to speak with our other half, to work out a better system or find out if there was any word on other locations to mine the stones. It has been some time, and he hasn't returned."

"So we would find this moving city and ask them where he is?" Valerie shrugged. "That seems easy enough."

"Unless they've hurt him, in which case they would then be your enemy and ours," Swarne interjected. "If that has happened, we all have a problem."

"Swarne!" Wokana scolded. "We shall not assume the worst. So, do we have a deal?"

Valerie couldn't see why not, so she agreed. They would go after the moving city, hope that Eran the sand snake god wouldn't eat them, and hope that he was still alive.

Although the storm was gone, the winds were still heavy and there was sand in the air. Luckily Valerie and Robin had brought their helmets in case there was trouble. Breathing air like this certainly qualified.

After slapping hers on Valerie glanced at Robin, who looked like a super space-warrior, a look that always made

Valerie want to laugh. Not that it was funny. It was terrifying, actually, and it didn't feel right for the young vampire she had rescued and taken under her wing.

Wind slashed at them, trying to push them back. Robin's voice came through the helmet's comm.

"Got that out of your system last night?"

"Sorry?" Valerie glanced over, almost wondering if she'd imagined it. "This is the time to talk about that?"

Robin stared forward, leaning into the wind. "We're out here alone. No chance for us to lose control with all this going on."

"True. Talk about sand in the butt," Valerie replied, then bit her lip. What a stupid thing to say. But then the realization hit her that Robin had just completely opened up to her, in a roundabout way. "You... You'd be tempted elsewhere?"

Silence followed.

More wind. More howling. A moving shadow in the distance that Valerie did her best to ignore.

"I don't want to lie to you, so I won't answer that." Robin turned her way, then forward again. "But what we talked about is still true. I want to concentrate; to not be distracted. To fight for the universe, and be a hundred percent focused on that and nothing else. Got it?"

"Yes." Valerie processed this, then shook her head. "But isn't ignoring it more distracting in a way?"

"Not for me," Robin replied.

Valerie nodded, though she was certain the action couldn't be seen. When they retraced their steps from the night before the large shadow was there again, albeit closer this time.

"Robin?"

Nothing.

The shadow moved toward them.

"Robin," Valerie picked up her pace, then turned to face Robin and pointed. "All that. Yes, okay, I'm sorry. I'll do my best, but right now we've got company."

Robin took a step away, then shouted, "*OH FUCK!*" and took off, with Valerie not far behind.

"Try to keep our sense of direction. Head for the ship as much as possible," Valerie told her. "We don't want to get lost in this!"

"How about we not die first, then worry about being lost?"

The ground beneath them shook, and the shadow rose into the air and loomed over them. No more playing around here. Valerie shouted for them to run, using all the energy within her. Full-on vampire mode took over, and she and Robin darted away as the sand snake plowed into the ground immediately behind them. The ground began to sink in, converging on the spot where the snake had landed, and a puff of sand joined the already heavy air.

They were off course, but Robin had a point about survival being their primary objective at the moment. Valerie continued to run, but spun in time to see the sand moving in waves toward them.

"There's more than one of them!" she shouted.

"Don't you fucking tell me that!" Robin replied, somehow moving even faster now. Valerie often forgot that Robin had been further enhanced on the ship, thanks to Bad Company. She was capable of much more than she had been on Earth.

Everything in Valerie told her not to look back again, but she couldn't help herself. She turned her head slightly and nearly stumbled at the sight of the sand erupting as a snake emerged, opening its three-way mouth to reveal rows upon rows of sharp teeth.

Well, shit. That idea of being stuck in an endless torture and healing process? It was a very real possibility.

Valerie pulled out her hip gun and shot like a mother-fucker as she ran, not letting up on the trigger or bothering to see if she was making contact. At the sound of gunfire and the roaring of the sand Robin went for her guns too, but before she pulled them out she pointed.

"There! We need to get over there!"

Valerie spun to see more dark shadows looming in the murky sky, and for a moment thought it might be more sand snakes. They weren't descending, though. The moving city!

She wanted to yelp with joy, but realized that seeing it wouldn't mean shit if she didn't live long enough to make it there.

"Remember earlier, with the explosion?" Valerie shouted into her comm.

"No fucking way!"

"You think we can outrun this thing? Think again."

"So what, then?" Robin's voice sounded panicked. "We kick off from each other and are on each side. What about the others?"

"Trust me," Valerie replied. "We're going to ride this bitch."

"I can't believe I'm going to do this." Robin turned

toward her and Valerie smiled, almost excited at the moment of near-death.

"*NOW!*"

Together they leaped as the sand snake came up behind them. The shadow of it was already on them as they brought their feet together like they had when avoiding the missiles from the Pallicon. They connected and clasped hands, then let go and kicked backward with all their might. Valerie felt the rush of air as the sand snake flew past. They cleared it—barely—and landed on their backs.

"Get up!" Valerie shouted, not checking to see if Robin obeyed. "Run toward me *now*."

The snake had started to sink back into the sand, but wasn't completely submerged yet. Valerie and Robin jumped onto its back, holding hands and balancing on its highest point as the sand snake plowed forward.

It accelerated in the direction of the moving city.

"It's got a new target," Robin stated, voice full of worry.

"The city?" Valerie asked, realizing that wasn't it as soon as the words left her mouth. With her enhanced sight she saw a small form running toward one of the massive metallic legs, but not fast enough. "Oh, come on!"

The sand snake dipped slightly, getting close to parallel with the ground, and Valerie debated what to do. She was about to tell Robin to let go when the sand snake leaped.

"Holy shittttt!" Robin screamed, her grip nearly squeezing Valerie's gloves right off.

They soared high into the air, almost able to see the upper portion of the moving city. For a moment the sand and everything else was gone, and all that mattered were the two vampire women flying blissfully through the sky.

Valerie let out a whoop of joy. "You don't get to do this back on Earth," she said triumphantly.

"Are you fucking nuts?" Robin screamed. "You're having fun right now? What the hell is wrong with you?"

Valerie looked at her and gave a crazy, excited laugh.

"We're going down." Robin laughed back. "Can you come back to reality for a moment and see how fucked we are?"

Valerie squeezed Robin's hands firmly. She stared at her through the helmet even though she couldn't see her and said in her most confident voice, "Trust me. We're strong; more powerful than you likely realize. Just...trust me."

No answer was forthcoming, just Robin's heavy breathing.

The ground came up fast, and Valerie could see that they were going to land on the figure down there. She couldn't see how it could escape.

But she had an idea.

"Don't let go," she said, using one hand to reach for her sword.

"What're you doing?"

"Just hold on to me!"

Valerie slammed her blade into the left side of the sand snake, but it barely penetrated at all. *Dammit.* She extracted it, and this time pulled Robin close and said, "Hands around my waist, now!"

Robin shrieked as Valerie pulled her other hand free, but the woman did as she was told. Using both hands, Valerie drove her sword into the sand snake's side with everything she had.

The sword bit deep and the creature shrieked and

spasmed, curling around the wound and hitting the ground off-target. The figure was able to leap to safety. Valerie and Robin were thrown free, but at least Valerie held onto her sword.

They rolled across the sand as the snake burrowed into the ground, but more mounds were moving toward them. Valerie leaped to her feet, ignoring the pain in her shoulder and hip since they'd be healed soon enough, and saw a female teenage Lavkin staring at them.

"Get out of here," Valerie shouted, drawing her pistol and opening fire on the oncoming sand snakes. Her shots disappeared into the ground to no effect.

"That won't work!" the teen shouted, motioning to them. "Come this way!"

Valerie hesitated, but those bastards were moving in fast. She and Robin followed the girl, who led them to a lever at the base of the closest metal leg of the moving city. The leg had secured itself to the ground with large spikes, and more cables shot out to anchor it at the sight of the oncoming sand snakes. A door opened and an adult Lavkin stood there with hand outstretched.

"Only the young female," the adult Lavkin shouted, pulling a curved gun on them.

"No," she shouted, pointing at the sand snake as it vanished into the ground. "They saved me. I'm not leaving them down here with those things!"

The adult cursed and glanced at Valerie and Robin, then lowered the gun and said, "Hurry, then!"

All three piled in with him, and at the push of a button they sped up an old rickety elevator through the leg. A

PRIME ENFORCER

blow shook the leg, then another, and Valerie and Robin froze, waiting for the whole thing to collapse.

"It'll hold," the girl told them. She motioned to her face, then pointed to theirs. "Hiding something?"

Valerie was the first to remove her helmet, then Robin.

"Not sure we're around friendlies yet," Valerie said with a curious look at the adult. "Are we?"

"Depends on you, and what you're doing here," he replied.

"I'm Valerie, and this is Robin." Valerie gave him a nod, as they'd done with Wokana. The male cocked his head, then bowed back.

"I'm Strop, and this is my daughter Lerra. Thank you for saving her."

"It was crazy," Lerra started excitedly. "They were riding one of them!"

"One of what?"

She lowered her voice now, as if saying something horrific. "Eran. Or one of the Eran."

Strop gazed at them with awe and terror, then dropped to one knee. "You...you have conquered them?"

"What?" Valerie shook her head. "We were simply surviving. That...that happened, but no, not conquered. Rode them, yes. Conquered, no."

He tilted his head, then stood again. "How? It-it's not possible, unless you are from the legends of old."

"Oh shit," Robin said, rolling her eyes. "Here we go with more religious mumbo-jumbo. Prophecies and all that."

"Robin!" Valerie chided.

"No, no," Strop said, holding up his hands to show that

no harm had been meant. "There are plenty of unbelievers here, so no offense taken. I myself am...undecided."

"But you were riding it. I saw you!" Lerra protested.

"My daughter is one of the more fervent believers," Strop said with a smile.

"And why not?" She turned to him, angry. "There has to be a life better than this. Always on the move, always at war with our own kind."

Strop bowed his head and the elevator clinked and clanged its way upward until it came to a stop. The doors opened and Strop let his daughter go first, then hesitated.

"What brings you here?"

"We need answers," Valerie replied. "About a certain Lavkin who goes by the name of 'Lolack.'"

The Lavkin's eyes widened, then he smiled. "I know Lolack very well. Have you found him?"

"He's not here then?" Robin asked.

Strop shook his head. "He was raised here. Came back to visit not long ago, actually. Now? We might be able to find some clues in his office, but that's all I can promise."

"Office?" Valerie glanced at Robin, hopeful. "He has an office here?"

"Yes. He set it up but only stayed for a couple of days before running off. He was excited about something or other, but as far as I've been able to gather, he didn't tell anyone more than that."

"We'd like to take a look."

Strop motioned for them to follow and led them into a metallic city with tall walls, guns mounted around the sides, and several Lavkins going about their business. The arrival of newcomers brought stares but Strop continued walking, guiding Valerie and Robin to a short tower at one end.

"In here, and be quick," he said. "You might not have much time."

"Will you get in trouble?" Valerie asked.

"They'll have questions, but we're all equals here. They are not my parents, after all, and we have no high priestess in this place."

"Thank you," Robin told him as she followed Valerie inside.

They wound their way up a staircase that emerged into what was no doubt the aforementioned office. It was a mess, complete with scribbles on the walls and various screens that Valerie guessed were attached to some sort of computer. She tried turning one on, but no luck.

"He went mad?" Valerie asked, shaking her head at all this.

"Over here," Robin called from the other side of the room. She knelt in the corner, tracing lines with her fingers. "I've always been fascinated by maps, and studied them when I could. This might be one."

Valerie couldn't see it at first, but then realized there was a pattern. Large circles had been drawn at specific points, squiggly lines at others.

"Was he..." Valerie followed the marks around the room, noticing that some of the squiggly lines were larger than others. "Yes, he was tracking the movement of the city relative to the locations of the sand snakes. There's a pattern to them!"

"Why would he care so much? To avoid them?"

"Maybe, but I'm not sure." Valerie focused on one

particular area with the circles drawn over themselves several times, right by a large square filled with squiggly lines. She ran to the stairs and hissed, "Strop, can you join us?"

A moment later he appeared, but he looked worried. "They want you out."

"Yes, fine," Valerie replied, pointing to the square. "The city, it's been here many times, no? Right here?"

He frowned. "I don't understand."

"Is there an area especially populated by the sand snakes? Erans?"

"Actually, yes. When Lolack was with us, we passed that particular area quite often. He kept going out, even though we warned him it was dangerous. But he always returned." He froze, looking confused. "Come to think of it, we hadn't gone very far the day he vanished. We were passing the scrapyards where we get parts to fix up the city. It might have been around there, though I can't understand why."

"Can you point us in the right direction?"

It was clear from Robin's expression that she didn't like the idea of traveling to a field of sand snakes, but she kept her mouth shut.

"If it means being rid of the two of you," Strop said, "the sooner the better. No offense meant."

"None taken," Valerie replied, beaming. They had made progress...or so she hoped.

CHAPTER SIXTEEN

Nearly one hundred Lavkins looked at Kalan, awaiting his instructions. They had gathered on the island for the training Kalan had promised to give them.

"Any idea what you're doing?" Bob asked him quietly.

"None at all." He cleared his throat and spoke loudly to the group. "Thank you all for coming. We're going to drill a few moves that might come in handy in the fight against the Wandarby cult. We don't have a lot of time so obviously I won't be able to cover anything too complicated, but if you do get into a hand-to-hand combat situation, there are a few things that are easy to learn and could save your life. Could I have two volunteers? Two people who feel pretty good about their hand-to-hand skills?"

After a bit of conversation and back and forth among the group, two males stepped forward. Both were above average height, and had a confident gleam in their eyes.

Kalan's plan was to use this time mostly to encourage them. He'd seen even during the gun fight on *Flamebird*'s observation deck that many of the Lavkins were more timid than he would have liked to see. They prided them-selves on their skills as pilots and marksmen, but became a bit nervous when things got up close and personal.

"Okay," he said when the two men stood in the cleared space in front of him. "I'd like you to spar. Your goal is to take the other person down. There are a lot of ways to kill an enemy once you get him on the ground, so let's start with learning how to get them there. When you're ready."

The two Lavkins circled each other, their eyes intent. One reached out with a long arm, but the other batted it away. One took a step forward, and the other took a step back. One gave a half-hearted kick, which the other easily dodged.

Kalan felt sick to his stomach watching them spar. This was going to be more difficult than he'd imagined. "Stop, please, before I fall asleep."

A light chuckle ran through the crowd.

Kalan thought a moment. "Let's do something different. Bob, Jilla, would you come up here and demonstrate, please?"

They immediately stepped forward and faced each other.

Bob smiled and said quietly. "Now that I know you have a crush on me, I'll take it easy on you."

Jilla's lips curled back in a snarl.

"Probably not a wise idea to provoke her," Kalan whis-pered. Then, loudly enough for the group to hear, "When you're ready."

The moment the words left his mouth Jilla charged, driving her shoulder into Bob's stomach and wrapping him up with her arms.

Bob responded just as quickly, bringing a sharp elbow down on her back, but Jilla didn't let go. She held him tightly, driving with her feet to push him backwards.

He almost fell over, but he grabbed her around the waist and lifted, then turned her upside down. Before he could slam her to the ground, she twisted and wrapped her legs around his neck. She unleashed three quick punches to his face, and he fell backward into the dirt.

As soon as his back touched the ground the match was over, so Jilla hopped off him and offered him her hand. She helped him up and patted him on the back. "Not bad, Bob."

Bob rubbed the red spot under his left eye where she'd hit him. "Thanks. You didn't do so bad yourself."

Kalan looked at the Lavkins, who were staring in shocked fascination, rattled by the unexpected ferocity of the sparring session.

"*That's* how you spar," he said. "You train that hard, you'll be used to putting yourself in the right mental state for a real fight. The Wandarby cultists think we are literally out to destroy the galaxy. Do you think they'll hold back in a fight? Now, give me two more volunteers to demonstrate a *real* sparring match."

No one responded; they just stared at him open-mouthed.

"I'll spar." It was Commander Larence. Kalan was impressed. The guy saw that his people needed someone to take the lead, so he was doing it.

"Excellent. We need one more volunteer."

"Actually," Larence said, "I was hoping I could spar with you, Kalan."

A murmur went through the crowd.

Now Kalan was really impressed. "All right. I'd be happy to spar with you."

The commander joined Kalan in the clearing. "Don't hold back," he said. "I won't."

The comment brought a smile to Kalan's face. "Fair enough. When you're ready."

Larence wasted no time in throwing a punch at Kalan's face. Kalan deflected it, but suddenly realized this fight was going to be more difficult than he'd thought. The Lavkin had at least four inches on him, and while he wasn't as powerful as Kalan, there was a kind of wiry strength behind that blow. He was fast, too.

Kalan needed to get in close. He feigned a left jab and then dipped right, ducking around the commander's defenses. Once in close, he threw a quick punch into Larence's stomach.

The air rushed out of the Lavkin, but he quickly regained it and snarled in anger. He drove a knee upward, catching Kalan in the stomach and driving him backward.

Larence attacked with his right hand next, but it was unlike any punch Kalan had ever seen. Instead of driving the fist forward with his shoulders and hips, Larence sort of flicked it at him. The long flexible arm reacted like a whip, unfurling and slapping Kalan hard in the face.

The commander snapped another right at him, then a left. Then another right. The blows were coming so quickly now and the Lavkin's reach was so impossibly long that Kalan couldn't get out of their way. He raised his arms to block and the left hand curled past them, catching him in the face.

He was reeling now, in real danger of toppling over. He

need to end this fast. Gathering his feet beneath him, he lunged forward and slammed into the Lavkin, wrapping him in his arms as Jilla had done to Bob. Kalan weighed twice as much as Jilla, though, and Larence was unable to stay upright. He tumbled to the ground.

The commander lay there for a moment panting, then a look of horror screwed up his face. "Holy hell. Kalan, I'm so sorry. I lost my temper. I never meant to—"

"Are you kidding me?" Kalan asked with a grin. "That was perfect." He held out a hand and helped the commander to his feet.

Larence brushed himself off. "That was... That was fun, actually."

"Feels good to cut loose now and again, doesn't it?" Kalan looked at the crowd, and was pleased to see that their looks of shock had been replaced with expressions of delight. "Let's hear it for Commander Larence. He's got one hell of a left hook."

The crowd erupted in cheers.

"You could have let Larence win," Bob whispered. "Might have boosted their spirits."

"They seem pretty boosted to me," Kalan said. "Besides, the whole point is to teach them not to hold back—to give their all in every situation. Taking it easy on Larence would have defeated that."

Commander Larence raised his hands, quieting the crowd. "All right, who's next?"

For the first time in more than a month, Kalan wedged himself into the cockpit of a fighter.

After watching the Lavkins spar for an hour, giving them pointers on their techniques and batting around some ideas on how they might use their long flexible arms in battle, Commander Larence had asked Kalan if he wanted to join him and some of the fighter pilots on a patrol exercise.

Since he couldn't fit in the narrow cockpits of the Lavkin fighters and lacked the conductive skin to operate them, he was using the Pallicon fighter Jilla and Wearl had stolen. As he started the ship, he felt calm flow over him. He hadn't piloted a ship since the Nim had crashed on the moon of Tol over a month ago, and hadn't realized until this moment how much he'd missed it.

He lifted off from the fighter's resting place on the island, and joined the six Lavkin fighters. Their aircraft were of a much more elegant design than the Pallicon craft he was piloting. It would be interesting to see how well they performed against one another.

Commander Larence's voice came through his headset. "You demonstrated your skills to us in the sparring matches, Kalan, but now it's time to show you where we truly excel. Come, we'll take you where pilots are made and pretenders are broken."

Kalan chuckled. "And here I thought we were just going for a friendly cruise. Lead the way, Commander."

Larence and the others banked hard to the west, and Kalan followed. The sky was a pale yellow, and so clear Kalan had an unobstructed view to the horizon.

"I've got one at the Henro Junction, Commander," a pilot said.

"Checking it," Larence said. Then, after a moment, "No, too small. We want to show Kalan the real thing."

"How about the one at Calla North?" another pilot offered.

There was a moment of silence, then Larence said, "A bit farther than I was hoping to travel, but I like the size of it. Lock on it."

Kalan wondered what they were talking about. Could it be some sea creature they wanted to show him? An especially large one, maybe? But they had said it would be a test of his piloting skills, so that didn't entirely make sense.

He resisted the urge to ask, sensing that to do so would be to fail the test before it even started.

The journey to the part of the sea they called Calla North took nearly an hour, and Kalan enjoyed the flight. The Lavkins were quiet most of the time, leaving him alone with his thoughts. He tried to absorb the moment, to push away all thoughts of the coming battle and what was likely to happen afterwards even if they survived. He cleared his mind of everything but the moment at hand. It was just him, his fighter, and the pale-yellow sky.

As they got closer to their destination, clouds began to build up. At first there were only a few billowing white clouds dotting the horizon, but soon their darker cousins began to occupy more of the expanse.

"It looks like we will be hitting some weather," he said into his headset.

That was met with a chorus of whoops.

"Uh, yeah, you could say that," Larence said with a laugh.

As the sky grew darker, Kalan began to understand where they were taking him and he felt his mouth go dry. "You guys are taking me into a hurricane, aren't you?"

"Ha, he got in it one!" someone shouted.

Kalan swallowed hard. "Isn't that a little, um, *dangerous?*"

"What happened to 'Give your all fearlessly,' Kalan?" Larence asked.

"Using my own words against me—not a cool move." He shifted in his seat and tightened his grip on the controls. "Okay, I'm game."

"Good, because it's too late to turn back now."

Moments later they entered the storm, and at first Kalan thought it wouldn't be too bad. This was no worse than other bad weather he'd flown through. But things were just getting started. The farther they went, the harder the wind and rain hammered the fighter. It suddenly seemed insane to be braving this weather wrapped in nothing but a small metal ship.

"A ship designed to withstand entering and leaving atmospheres," he muttered to himself. "This is nothing."

The wind grew more powerful.

"We're about the enter the eyewall," Larence shouted through the headset. "This is the strongest part of the storm!"

Kalan gritted his teeth. He'd really been hoping the most difficult part was behind them.

The storm was so thick around him now that all he could see outside the ship was a gray haze and the ship rattled in the violent wind—a disconcerting sound he'd never heard in a fighter. He hit a gust, and was lifted out of his seat as the plane dipped. Thankfully the harness over his shoulders stopped his rise after only a couple inches, and he quickly dropped back into his seat.

He gripped the controls, hoping against hope that this fighter he'd never flown before today would stay together in the storm. Why had the Lavkins brought him here? Did they have some kind of death wish?

Then he abruptly broke through the eyewall, and everything was still. The change was so sudden, so unexpected, that it took his breath away.

"Woo!" Larence cheered him over the headset. "You did it, brother! You made it through. Welcome to the eye of the storm."

He could see the clouds swirling on every side of him, but here the sky was clear. All he heard was the dull rumble of his engine. He let out a relieved laugh. "This is amazing!"

"I know," Larence answered. "This is why we do it. To prove to ourselves we can face down the toughest storm there is, survive one hundred and twenty mile-an-hour winds, to get to this. The tranquility at the eye of the hurricane."

Kalan had to admit that he'd never experienced anything quite like this. "Thank you, Larence. Thanks for bringing me here."

"No problem." He paused for a moment. "Have you realized yet that we're going to have to fly through it again to get home?"

Kalan chuckled. That had crossed his mind, but for now he just wanted to enjoy the calm.

CHAPTER SEVENTEEN

The sky was far less hazy now; they could even see the sun. That might mean less interference, Valerie figured, so she tried her comm again as they made their way toward what she imagined would be a hive of massive sand snakes.

"Val, is that you?" Garcia answered on the third try. "We were getting worried! Where are you?"

"Listen, can you put a tracker on us? Maybe start heading toward us, but with caution?"

Garcia hesitated. "Sounds like you're in trouble."

"We don't know yet, but we aren't exactly sure where the ship is from our location. Can you do it?"

"Of course we can." Garcia shouted to the others that Valerie was on the comm, and Flynn and Arlay were on a second later, asking her all about their journey so far.

"Were you stuck in the storm?"

"Wasn't it insane?"

"Did you meet any aliens? Any luck on the Lolack front?"

"Okay, okay," Valerie said, interrupting them. "We think

we're on the right track, but I'll fill you in when we're back on the ship."

"Roger that," Garcia said. "We'll start pinging your location. Hope to see you soon."

"Perfect," she replied. "But remember, proceed with caution. I don't need the ship being attacked by the monsters out here."

"Um, monsters?"

"Giant sand snakes, or sand worms—whatever you want to call them."

"And you'll be all right?"

"I doubt it," Robin muttered into her comm. "Oh, sorry! I didn't mean to say that out loud."

"Val," Garcia said, "if you're in trouble, we can just get out of here. Better to have you two alive and fighting the good fight than lose you. That would be the end of our journey."

"We'll figure it out, Garcia." Valerie glanced at Robin. The younger woman couldn't see the scowl through her helmet, but she hoped she felt it. "Thank you for the worry though. It's touching."

"Tell you what," Robin said, clearly trying to sound chipper. "If it comes down to it, I'll sacrifice myself so Valerie can live to see another day. No worries, I got this."

"Not funny," Valerie and Garcia said in unison.

"Right, sorry. But I would."

"I know," Valerie replied, "but I'd do the same for you and I'm faster, so there."

"Val, if you ever die in my place, I'll come after you and kick your fat ass."

Snickers from the comm.

"Excuse me?" Valerie said, now slightly annoyed. "I do *not* have a fat ass."

"Didn't you say the enhancements Michael gave you back in Old Manhattan…the ones that allowed you to walk in the daylight. Didn't you say those made your breasts bigger?" Robin was clearly teasing her now, but Valerie found her irritation growing. On the other hand, the younger woman seemed to have nearly forgotten her worry over the sand snakes.

"What's your point?" Valerie countered.

"It follows that your ass would've grown bigger too. You know, as a counterbalance."

"What the fuck? Garcia, Flynn, cover your ears."

Robin laughed. "Oh, come on… As if they haven't noticed that badonkadonk going on back there. I mean, don't get me wrong…" Robin leaned back to take a look, "it's ni-iice."

"Oh my God!"

"You do have a nice rear end," Garcia said. "You know, as a professional ass-lover to a friend."

"First of all, we work together," Valerie said back to him. "I would think this is in some way inappropriate. What if we were all commenting on how large your twig and berries got after your Pod time?"

"Ummm…"

"Agh, bad example." Valerie went on, "As if anyone can see my ass in this armor anyway."

"You can't see my twig and berries in mine," Garcia countered. "Although I do think the Pod—"

"Enough, enough." Arlay cut them off. "Are you all a

bunch of teenagers? On my planet, only teenagers speak like this."

Silence followed, then Garcia burst into laughter. Valerie couldn't help but join in.

"Actually, on Earth it's teenagers and pretty much everyone in the military," Garcia answered the question. "Maybe the fact that we could lose our lives any day means we don't watch what we say as much. Just enjoy life and all that."

"Or maybe your lack of a regular sex life means you're all as horny as Skulla, and, yes, they have that reputation. Maybe you need to get some."

A long silence followed.

"Um, still there, guys?" Valerie asked. "Do we need to tell Flynn to close his eyes? I'd hate to hear his innocence has been stripped by you two."

The image of Garcia running his hand over Arlay's tentacles flashed through Valerie's mind, and she couldn't help but shudder in disgust. Was that racist of her? Species-ist? Back on Earth such concepts had largely vanished, but then again, on Earth nobody had tentacles on their skin-like hair.

"We're here," Garcia said, voice much more edgy. "Something's going on with the ship. We're moving toward you, and I see something in the distance to the left of where it shows your location. Maybe a city?"

"Another city?" Valerie asked, curiously glancing about but not seeing anything.

"I can't be certain that's what it is, but... We'll try to contact..."

Static interrupted his voice, and the comm stopped working.

"You still hear me, right?" Valerie asked, turning to Robin.

"Loud and clear."

"You got all silent for a moment. Everything okay?"

"It's just... No, it's stupid."

"What?" Valerie protested. "Come on."

"Well, all this talk of enhancements...and let's be honest, we've all seen Garcia after a shower—I have to imagine that was due to the Pod enhancements. Everyone but me, huh?"

"I'm not following. You...oh!"

"Yeah, I mean how come your enhancements affected you that way, and his—you know—but my tits are the same size?"

"I'm not sure how comfortable I am with this conversation, considering where we ended things last night."

Robin sighed. "Just wondering, is all."

An image of Robin bathing in a river on their way north along the East Coast of America flashed through Valerie's mind.

"Better for fighting, you realize that? Plus, your breasts are perfect. I mean, objectively speaking, perfect for fighting. You don't want too much stuff flying around."

"Well, the armor would hold that in place." Robin added, "You're right, of course. I just...wasn't sure why I hadn't noticed a difference. And which one is objectively again?"

Valerie smiled, remembering that Robin had been raised in the badlands of America. Her education hadn't been the same as among an elite group of vampires in Old France, like Valerie.

"Well, the other is 'subjectively,' which you can remember by thinking of it like it's the subject's point of view, or opinion."

"That's actually logical, unlike so much of our stupid language."

Valerie laughed. "You walk around here, fighting and barely surviving sometimes, and you're focusing on what you don't like about our language?"

"We have down time. What do *you* think about?"

"Hmmm." Valerie thought back to Sandra and Diego raising their baby in New York, to Micky and the others and all the fighting they'd gone through with her, and then moments lying on the ship and remembering how it felt to have flesh pressed against hers. At times her mind went to Robin, and at others back to Jackson, her lover before her short exploratory stint with Robin. Instead of explaining all that she simply said, "The old days, and wondering what comes next. When this is over here, what then?"

"Like, will we go back to Earth?" Robin continued walking and glancing around as the storms picked up in the distance. "I want to go back for sure, but I also want to be certain there's no more threat out here."

"So, back to the Federation? Check in with Nathan and see about fighting at Bethany Anne's side or something?"

"I guess so, yeah." Robin chuckled. "I mean, anywhere they want, but can you imagine charging into battle with the legendary BA?"

"We keep this up, imagine how many out there will

someday say the same about you. 'Imagine running into battle with Robin at your side!'"

"Pssh, they'll talk about *you*," Robin protested. "Me? They'll talk about me like some sidekick, I bet. The great Valerie and her sidekick Robin."

"Nah, Robin isn't a sidekick kind of name. That's a hero right there. A legend."

"You think?"

"Shit, have you ever seen a robin?" Valerie asked. "I mean the bird."

"No, actually."

"I did once." She remembered the way it had landed on a grassy field and held its beak high, assessing its surroundings like it owned the place. Birds were rare on Earth after the World's Worst Day Ever (WWDE), so it was a treasure to see one. "It was amazing the way it stood there, its orange breast striking against the green grass. One thing I remember—it had authority, just like you. Nobody was going to mess with that bird."

No answer came for a moment, then Robin said, "Thank you."

"Of course, when I ate it—"

Robin hit her in the shoulder, her metallic glove clanging on the body armor.

"Joking, joking," Valerie said with a laugh.

"Not the time for jokes," Robin said, slapping her shoulder again, but this time to get her attention as she pointed ahead.

The sand was rippling again, and then the vibrations hit. Valerie stepped closer to her friend, knees bent and ready to move. With an explosion of clay and sand, three sand snakes burst forth. Much smaller than the ones from before, but still about the size of the *Grandeur*.

Robin backed up farther, but then more vibrations shook the ground, followed by hundreds of these smaller sand snakes coming across the field—and at the other side of it Valerie saw why. Something was moving over there, with a red glow to it.

With her enhanced vision she could barely make it out, but it seemed to be some sort of vehicle.

"Somebody is over there," Valerie said.

"We're not crossing this!"

"Watch me," Valerie said, and started sprinting. Instantly the ground in front of her opened, sinking into a massive sand snake's mouth.

Robin pulled her back, shouting in frustration, "Dammit, Val! You're going to get yourself killed, and kill me with a heart attack at the same time."

Valerie's chest felt like it was going to implode, but she wasn't giving up so easily. Between breaths she managed to say, "We're going to see what that is. If it's him, we can't leave it like this."

"*Fuck!*" Robin shouted, kicking the sand in front of her.

Valerie saw movement at the same time as she acted, tackling Robin out of the way as a small sand snake dove past them.

"We could just turn around and leave all this behind," Robin said, "but we're not doing that, are we?"

"No way in hell."

"That's what I thought you'd say. Well then, come on. I figure our best bet is to run like crazy-ass motherfuckers, dodging and weaving... Rolling, maybe. Whatever it takes to stay out of their way, and not let them find a pattern in our movements."

"That's all you've got? Run like crazy bitches?" Valerie laughed. "I love it."

"On the count of one," Robin said. "One!"

They took off, running exactly as she had described, and it was fun as hell. Even Robin was laughing as she rolled past Valerie, then sprang to her feet and dodged left, doing a cartwheel before leaping like a ballerina.

"This is so stupid!" Valerie shouted, cracking up before she could say anything else. After a pirouette of her own she added, "And I can't believe it's working!"

"Believe it, girl. I might not be as educated as you are, but I've got ideas."

"Or you're insane."

"Both might indeed apply," Robin countered with a laugh.

After the next jump Valerie landed in a roll, coming up right on the other side of a sand snake, then twisted as another jumped between her and the last.

"I think they're catching on," Valerie said.

"Well, it doesn't matter," Robin countered. "We're almost there!"

Sure enough, between their vampire speed and losing themselves in the excitement of the moment, they'd nearly crossed the whole area. Now the vehicle was clearly in sight, but the driver had noticed them too, and was retreating to the hills beyond, toward what they could now see was a small cave.

"Come here!" Valerie shouted, charging after him.

However, she forgot about the crazy moves, and three

sand snakes picked up her trail and converged on her. One leaped and she tried to dodge, but it slammed into her. Only a baby, this one was about her size, but its teeth tried to tear into her body armor as the other two went for her.

Robin was on her then, the two rolling and the first sand snake with them, then Valerie got ahold of it and slung it back toward the others. The cave was just ahead, so they both sprang up and sprinted for it, not bothering to look back.

When they heard the clanking of their metal boots on rock a wave of relief came over them, but they still dove into the cave just in case. Valerie's eyes scanned the small area for the figure they hoped would be Lolack. A green light shone first, then they heard some sort of alien plasma gun charging, and out he stepped. There was no question— this was Admiral Lolack. He was tall; an orange-skinned Lavkin like the others here, but aged and battle-hardened, as evidenced by the look in his eyes.

"You have until I pull the trigger to tell me who you are and what you're doing here," he said, stepping forward so they could see him better.

"We're in need of the Lost Fleet," Valerie said.

"The Lost…" He chuckled. "You do realize it had a name before it was the Lost Fleet, right? I think what you mean is you're looking for *Lolack's* Fleet. Well, you've found Lolack —that's me. But as you can see, I have no fleet."

"And if we told you we not only know where your fleet is—or a good portion of it—but that your galaxy needs you?"

"I'm done with all that. I'm a simple farmer now."

Valerie frowned, glancing around as if she had missed something. "A farmer?"

"The sand snakes, yes." He blushed. "I've been doing research, and it turns out their droppings are quite fertile. They can be used for growing food... Other plants too. They'll change this whole planet."

"You're kidding," Robin protested. "You don't want to help save the universe because you're busy harvesting snake shit?"

He scowled at her. "What could be so dangerous out there anyhow? You two can handle it, I'm sure. You managed to survive down here, and to find me."

"There's an AI called Aranaught," Valerie started, watching as his face contorted at that pronouncement. "Not only is she after the fleet, she means to take on the whole galaxy, and then the universe."

"Some imagination you kids have," Lolack growled. "And I'm supposed to believe all this? We disbanded the fleet, okay? I gave all that up."

"Arlay is with us. She says she knows you."

His scowl instantly faded at that name, and he lowered his gun. "Arlay? She's here?"

"Not far away, actually. With the ship. She wasn't sure if you'd remember—"

"Of course I do." He holstered the gun, then nodded firmly. "Take me to her. Now."

Valerie and Robin glanced at each other, pleased with how that went, but then remembered the danger outside.

"And the snakes?" Valerie asked.

Lolack grinned and turned to the vehicle he had driven on the way in. When he kicked it the machine turned on, sputtering and vibrating and emitting an eerie red glow from the bottom.

"The vibrations make the snakes think I'm one of them," he said proudly. "Best way to ride around out there and enjoy their beauty."

"Oh, God," Robin protested. "You're as crazy as Val."

He laughed. "We'll see about that. But if Arlay isn't really with you and this is all a trick, I can be very nasty."

"It's not a trick," Valerie said. "And we're very aware of your reputation. That's why we're here, remember?"

He humphed, then slid into the driver's seat and waited while Valerie and Robin arranged themselves in the back. In a way it felt like a floating stage, or like a chariot without wheels or a horse.

"Ready?" Lolack asked. "Point me in the right direction and we'll be there in no time. This baby really moves."

They said they were, and he maneuvered the machine back out of the cave and into the field of sand snakes. Before there had been a few, but now they were everywhere, jumping through the sky and wriggling along the ground. How Robin couldn't see the beauty in them was beyond Valerie.

Lolack glanced back and Valerie pointed, so he pushed the machine in the direction indicated, tearing past the alien reptiles. They were finally on their way back to the *Grandeur*.

CHAPTER EIGHTEEN

A cool wind blew across the water, chilling Kalan's skin as he made his way along the metal walkways between the various ships and the island.

He and Wearl were exploring, hoping to walk the entire length of the walkways. It had occurred to him that he hadn't spent much time anywhere except *Flamebird* and the island in his time on Rewot. When the Wandarby came he didn't want to be caught in a chase and have no idea where he was going, so they walked.

As they did, Kalan found his mind going to the Shimmers and their culture. Despite spending his first eighteen years among them, he really didn't know that much about how they lived. "Tell me about the Shimmers, Wearl."

She made a strange humming noise he took to be pensive. "What do you want to know?"

"Anything. What do you beings do when you're not guarding prisoners on SEDE or fighting for Valerie's Elites? What's your home planet like? Do you have sports? Religion? Holidays?"

"I'll answer that last one first," she said. "Our most important holiday is Urggle's Day." She made a strange gurgling sound as she said it.

"I'm sorry, 'Urggle's Day?'"

She chuckled. "Close enough. Urggle's Day takes place in the darkest time of the year, a time when we only have light for about hour a day, but we spend the rest of the year preparing for it. Each Shimmer is expected to bring a gift of great worth. For some, that means they save money all year so they can buy a piece of jewelry or an electronic device for the holiday. Others spend all year creating something. They may build something with their own two hands, or pay an artist to create something. What matters is that the person sees the gift as having great value."

"And then you give that to someone?" Kalan guessed. "Your parent, maybe?"

"Not exactly. On the evening of Urggle's Day, all the Shimmers come to the center of town and sing Urggle's Day songs and tell tales of Urggle's heroics. Then we find a stranger, someone we've never seen before, and present them with our gift. It is meant to remind us that the sacrifices we make for Shimmers we've never met are just as important as the ones we make for our families."

They reached another ship, *Havertt's Son*, and turned left onto another metal walkway.

"Wow, Wearl. That's actually really sweet. I guess Shimmers have a soft side after all."

"Perhaps we do," she admitted.

"Who was Urggle, anyway?"

Wearl sounded ever more excited when she spoke again. "Oh, she's much more than just the basis for the holiday. Her most famous deed is the bloodletting of Gavun, of course. She and her army dismembered an entire city in a single afternoon. Remarkable stuff!"

"Er, yeah, remarkable," Kalan said, shaking his head. That sounded more like the Shimmers he was familiar with. "One more question. What exactly do you look like?"

He felt a bit awkward asking the question, especially after having traveled with her for nearly two months now. It felt like something he should have asked long ago.

"Hmm, it's difficult to put into words," she answered. "Technically things look like how you perceive them with your eyes, so I guess I look like nothing. At least to the eyes of most beings in the galaxy. There is a way you could see me, though."

He tilted his head. "Really? Like the way you reprogrammed my translation chip to be able to hear you?"

"Sort of. This procedure would be a little more invasive. I'd have to pluck out your eyes and replace them with specially-programmed cybernetic ones. I figured we should at least discuss it before I took that step."

Kalan's eyes widened. "I think I'll pass on that one for now."

"I thought as much." She sighed. "There is one other way to see me though. With your hands."

He considered that for a moment. In their time together he'd brushed against Wearl plenty of times, but he'd never really touched her, at least not purposely.

"All right." He stopped walking and turned to face her.

Something warm grabbed his hand and raised it.

And then his fingers brushed against skin. It was soft, but oddly ridged. He moved his hand a little and realized he was touching her face. He felt her ridged cheeks. The hard ridge of her nose. Soft lips. His fingers lingered over those for a moment.

Wearl tensed suddenly. "What is that? Behind you."

Kalan pulled his hand away and turned. A figure had climbed out of the water and onto the walkway. "What the hell?"

He marched toward the figure, who had his back to him.

"Hey," Kalan called. "What are you doing?"

The being turned, and Kalan was surprised to see it was Commander Larence.

Larence seemed positively shocked to see Kalan and gave him a long look, as if appraising him for the first time.

"I didn't expect to see you out here," Kalan said. "Why were you in the water?"

Larence grinned sheepishly. "Don't tell anyone, but I fell in. My mind was elsewhere, and I slipped. Tumbled over the railing."

"That's a lie," Wearl growled, "and a lame one, too."

Kalan agreed with her assessment, but since Larence couldn't hear Wearl he decided to play it cool a little longer. He had a theory he wanted to check. "Oh wow, that's crazy. I'm glad you're all right."

"Me too," Larence chuckled. "I'm more embarrassed than anything. Like I said, I'd really appreciate it if you wouldn't spread it around."

"Of course not," Kalan agreed. His eyes fixed on a single strand of the man's hair, and then he saw it: the hair flickered. Kalan resisted the urge to grab the commander by the throat. "That was some boat ride we went on earlier. I can't believe we didn't capsize."

Larence laughed nervously. "Same here. That was crazy."

Kalan smiled. "Here's the thing, 'Larence...' We didn't go on a boat ride earlier. I know you're a Pallicon."

The false commander shook his head. "That's not true. Where would you even get an idea like that?"

"I've heard that if you inflict enough pain on a Pallicon, it reverts to its true form. Your kind can't help it—it's like a reflex or something. Shall we put the theory to the test?"

The creature glared at him for a moment, then shifted to his Pallicon form.

Kalan grabbed his arm. "How many more of you are down here?"

"Hundreds," he said defiantly. "We've infiltrated your entire fleet."

"He's alone," Wearl observed. "If he weren't, he'd be trying to protect his friends by saying he was alone."

"I agree with that assessment," Kalan said.

The Pallicon blinked hard. "Who are you talking to?"

Kalan ignored the question. "Come with me. I'm going to introduce you to the leaders of this squadron, and we're going to have a little chat."

The enemy Pallicon sat in a chair, surrounded by Mej, Lien, and Kalan. They hadn't tied him down, and they didn't need to. Mej and Lien could be intimidating presences when they wanted to be, and right now they definitely did.

"Let's start with something simple," Mej ordered, her voice cold. "Tell us your name."

The Pallicon said nothing.

Mej kept her eyes fixed on him. "Kalan, would you mind removing one of his fingers?"

"Irem," the Pallicon said quickly. "My name is Irem."

"See, that wasn't so difficult," Mej said with a smile. "The form you took… Where did you see it?"

It was a good question. In order to copy Commander Larence's form so accurately, the Pallicon would have needed to see him up close.

"Footage from one of our transports during the most recent attack. A camera caught him on top of a ship, fighting our troops. He looked important."

That must have been when Kalan had been down on the observation deck helping Jilla prepare to infiltrate the Wandarby cult, Kalan realized.

Still, it had been a stupid move on Irem's part. The beauty of the Lavkins' way of life was that they were so close to everyone around them, it would be almost impossible for a Pallicon to replace one of their people without being noticed.

"Why did you come?" Mej asked.

The Pallicon nodded toward Kalan. "He dragged me here."

"Don't be an idiot," Lien growled. "You know what she means."

Irem hesitated, so Kalan leaned forward and started inspecting his fingers as if selecting one to remove.

The Pallicon pulled his fingers away and nodded toward Kalan. "I was sent to validate his existence."

Mej and Kalan exchanged a glance. That didn't make much sense.

"Why?" Mej asked. "Your people saw him during the attack, did they not?"

Irem's lips tightened into a thin line.

"Fingers," Kalan said in a sing-song voice.

"The local temple saw him," Irem said, "but I work for the High Priest."

"You're going to have to explain that," Lien ordered.

Irem sighed and looked at them like they were idiots. "The Wandarby Church of Truth is divided into temples. Each temple has a warship and a squadron of fighters and each reports to the High Priest, the ultimate authority among the Wandarby. Your local temple became fixated on the Lavkins, and the idea that you were hiding Bandians in your midst. The rest of us were skeptical, so when they contacted the High Priest to report they'd seen one of you and request the military support of the whole church, he didn't believe them. He sent me to check the rumor out."

Kalan thought about that for a moment. If the majority of the Wandarby cult didn't believe he was here, they could use that to their advantage. Perhaps they could find a way to convince this High Priest that the local temple was crazy.

"Let me ask you something," Kalan said to the Pallicon. "Why do you hate Bandians so much? Did my grandmother trip your grandmother going down the stairs or something?"

Irem let out a humorless laugh. "As if you didn't know."

"Humor me," Kalan ordered.

"Fine." Irem leaned forward, glaring at Kalan. "The sacred texts tell of a time when the universe was young. All peoples lived in peace back then. The Pallicons. The Skulla. Countless others. Even the Lavkins. We all helped one another, and sought to advance our societies. Space travel was new then, and we freely shared our scientific discoveries. We believed that a win for one species was a win for all. Then we discovered a new planet—the home of the Bandians."

Kalan tilted his head at that. Was there really such a planet? Was it possible there were still Bandians living there today?

Irem continued, warming up to his story now. "At first the Bandians seemed friendly enough. They weren't as advanced, of course, and they were as dim-witted then as they are today, but they were skilled at hiding their evil intentions. There was one female among the Pallicon who had a vision. Her name was Wandarb, and she saw the truth: the Bandians were destined to smother all light in the universe. At first everyone thought she was crazy, but her words soon proved prophetic."

"That so?" Kalan asked. "Funny, it seems like there's still light in the universe to me."

Irem frowned. "For now. Thanks to the few who are brave enough to defend it."

"Like you?"

The Pallicon didn't answer. Instead, he went back to his tale. "The Bandians were eager to learn, despite their natural stupidity. It turned out they were as determined as they were dumb. They worked hard to grasp the concepts behind spaceship design, and studied the sciences better races had brought to their world until they had mastered them. When they had learned all they could, they killed every alien being on their planet. From there they spread out, and their intentions became clear. They wished to be the only species left, at which time they would even kill themselves. They wish to see all life in the universe snuffed out permanently."

Kalan chuckled. "Tell me something, Irem... If the Bandians are so big and evil, why are there so few of us left?"

Irem smiled in response to that. "Because of the bravery of the followers of Wandarb. We've given up everything to see your kind die, and soon you will join your dead kin."

Mej leaned forward. "So now the High Priest wants confirmation. Once that happens, he'll call in the other Wandarby temples and their warships?"

"You misunderstand," Irem said with a grin. "The temples have already gathered. They are in orbit above Rewot now. When the High Priest has confirmation, he will order the attack. And, having seen your little setup here on the water, I feel comfortable saying it will not be a long battle. You will be crushed until all that's left is the dust of your bones. Your only chance is to hand over the Bandian and beg for mercy."

Lien crossed his arms. "We're not big on begging for mercy around here, or on handing our brothers to their enemies."

"It's a real shame you weren't able to confirm the existence of the Bandian for the High Priest," Mej said. "Guess he'll have to send another spy."

Irem chuckled. "I'm afraid you're wrong there." He reached into his pocket and pulled out a small electronic device. "I sent the confirmation as soon as I saw the Bandian standing on the walkway. While we've been sitting here talking about my fingers, the High Priest has been preparing his attack."

At that moment, a Lavkin stuck his head through the door. "Mej, we need you."

"Not now," she snapped.

"It's important. We received a communication from someone calling himself the High Priest. He wants to talk."

CHAPTER NINETEEN

"You say you last heard from them from this direction, and they said they saw a city?" Lolack asked, glancing back at them skeptically.

"They weren't sure it was a city, but—"

"The scrapyard, then," Lolack cut in. "That could possibly look like a city. But communications cutting out—that's fairly normal around here."

"It was clear at the time," Robin interjected. "Not sure if that matters."

He glanced up at the sky, which was nowhere near clear at the moment, and shrugged. "Try them again."

Valerie called her companions' names, but got no response.

"The scrapyard is there," he said, pointing to a dark line on the horizon. "The term isn't exactly accurate, since locals live there and keep it moving. A sort of electric city, mostly below ground level. They were here long before the Lavkins set up a colony, and will be here long after we're gone."

"How can you be so sure?" Valerie asked.

"Because they aren't like us. They were made by an ancient race, someone from long ago, and—"

"Wait, made? Like robots?"

He nodded. "Yes. Why does that cause your voice to get all shaky-like?"

"Here's the part we need to fill you in on. The AI that moved out had a whole army at its disposal, and it can travel fast, taking over ships, space stations, and—"

"Robots," he said, eyes going wide at the idea.

"They have our friends, don't they?" Robin asked. The tone of her voice showed she had no doubts about the answer to that question.

"Looks like I'm back on the job," Lolack said, suddenly turning the machine around.

"What're you doing?" Valerie asked. "Our friends are that way."

"And you want to simply ride in and demand them back?"

"You have a better plan, I'm guessing."

"Indeed I do." He turned to the sun, glancing around and getting his directions down, then steered slightly more to the left. "The sand snakes."

"You're going to ask the sand snakes for help?" Valerie felt her jaw go slack at the thought.

He grinned. "I've been studying them, learning how to move them around like you do back on Earth. I am the sheep dog, they are my sheep."

"The light?" Robin asked, and Valerie realized it too. They had seen the most sand snakes when it was clearest out, except for the largest ones.

"They're attracted to it," he said. "And especially this one. Observe."

Already the ground was beginning to shift. When the forms of sand snakes showed through, he pressed a button so that the red light illuminated the sand beneath them.

"Be ready to jump," he said.

"Jump?"

He nodded, then turned the machine and sped back in the direction of the scrapyard. Many snakes followed, with more joining them along the way.

"Why are we jumping exactly?" Valerie asked.

"Because we want to be in the tunnel when the rest of them hit the scrapyard."

"In the tunnel?" Robin shook her head. "Why do I not like the sound of that?"

"Because it's the tunnel of a sand snake and we'll have to move fast, before the dirt buries us alive. Think you're up for it?"

"We haven't backed down from anything yet," Valerie replied.

He grinned back at them, showing them perhaps their first crazy Lavkin. Beyond him, the thin line on the horizon had morphed into walls and piles of metal, and drones appeared overhead. Several robots were at a wall, staring outward.

"Not yet?" Robin asked.

Lolack shook his head, turning to watch the ground. "We're waiting for her."

"Her?"

"*HER!*" He stepped back, pointing down. A quick glance showed the sands rippling with the movements of a sand snake that could only be the main one—the one she had seen in the storm the night before. "Now!"

He thrust a lever on the machine forward and ran past them, then jumped.

"I'll admit it is kinda fun!" Robin said, and went after him.

Valerie stared in horror as they hit the sand. It gave way to a tunnel following the sand snake, then quickly started to fill with sand. Robin and Lolack were running behind the snake, Robin pulling him along. While the Lavkins could move fast with their long legs, it wasn't fast enough. Valerie jumped now too, spinning as she fell so that she was able to follow them and roll into it, coming out of the roll already running.

"This is our kind of crazy," Valerie shouted, looking at the sand piling in behind them and the massive tail of the sand snake ahead.

"Fuck yeah!" Robin shouted, pumping her free fist in the air as her other hand pulled Lolack aside.

The sand snake dove and then leaped into the air—and they saw the metal wall, the drones, and more sand snakes plowing through the ground as the machine above slammed into one of the walls and pieces scattered.

"Keep moving!" Lolack shouted, pointing to the other tunnels the sand snakes were leaving. They narrowly got to another as the first collapsed, before moving up to the wall and passing through a newly made tunnel directly beneath it.

"Now what?" Valerie asked, realizing they were beneath the scrapyard.

"As I said, it's mostly underground, so..." He gestured

ahead just as a sand snake burst into open space, crashing through sheets of metal and piles of junk and sliding to a stop on the ground before writhing across the rubble.

Valerie was quick to act, leaping to Robin's side and helping her pull Lolack along, and then the three were on an opposite ledge of metal and ducking into the chambers left in the rumble by the snake's passage. More sand snakes plowed through above them and past them, Lolack cringing at each one.

Each clang of a snake against metal was accompanied by new alarms sounding, and Valerie felt her heart pounding through her skull at the threat of the next snake slamming into her. The ledge jolted; a support beam likely going out. Robin grabbed Valerie, holding her tightly, and Valerie grabbed Lolack. They would fall if one more jolt hit the walls, but it didn't happen, and soon the sounds came to a stop. All that remained were the alarms and the whirring of drones.

When it was over, Lolack finally relaxed.

"I hope none of them were hurt," he whispered worriedly, eyes narrowed.

"The sand snakes?" Valerie hissed.

He nodded. "They're just local wildlife—nothing we should want hurt. And in this case, they served as the first step of this rescue attempt."

"And the second step?" Robin asked.

Lolack grinned. "I was an admiral, not a miracle worker. That part's up to you."

Valerie turned to him with shock. "You threw us in here like this without any more to the plan?"

"Hey, you wanted a ride to the front door. We're at least one step farther than *you* would have been."

Valerie had to give him that, and clamped a hand over her mouth to keep herself from saying anything more as drones whirred closer to assess the damage. After they had gone on, Robin was the first to speak.

"There's only one thing we're really good at in times like this." She licked her lips, hand on her pistol. "We'll shoot our way out. Sometimes we punch and kick too, and maybe bite an ear or two."

"But since we're fighting an AI…" Valerie scrunched her nose.

"We don't need to fight it if we can find your friends and break them free, am I right?" Lolack asked.

"Correct."

"Great, then let's do that."

Valerie liked his confidence. She agreed, glancing around. "This feels like a maze."

He nodded. "It's their categorization and storage system. I've been here many times looking for the right part. Most of the robots were designed to organize and categorize, so we won't be seeing missiles or machine guns on them, but we should still be careful."

"Copy that."

"Where would they be most likely to keep our friends?" Robin asked.

He considered this, then his face lit up. "I'm guessing they came in a ship?"

"How else would we have flown here?"

"Yes," Valerie said, hoping he didn't notice Robin's sarcasm.

Lolack didn't seem to care, just waved for them to follow him as he ducked through a partially-crushed passage back into the catacombs. Wires were sparking and walkways were falling in on themselves, likely the areas set up for the Lavkins to walk through and find the parts they came for. It would take a while to fix it all back up, Valerie imagined.

And then something moved.

A small red dot, on and off... Moving now, turning green and following them.

The ruse was over.

"Faster," Valerie said, already picking up the pace. "We're not alone anymore."

As soon as she said it, robots clanged on the ledges nearby, metal sliding as they moved.

A voice spoke above it all. "It's so good to see you again, Valerie."

"Aranaught," Valerie replied, eyes darting around as she realized she was essentially surrounded by her enemy.

"Imagine my pleasure when first your ship sails right to me, and then you walk in." Aranaught laughed, and before she was even done the surge of the attack came. Drones opened fire as worker bots came for them, and Lolack threw himself to the ground as Valerie and Robin moved to meet the attack.

Valerie found openings to dive through so she could come out swinging, knocking a drone into the far wall and then turning it on the worker bots and other drones, still firing. She tossed it away so that it exploded on the far side, but the whole area shuddered again and Lolack screamed, "Don't make it fall and crush us!"

Robin was causing a commotion behind her, firing into the worker bots. More blinking lights came on, and a series of drones flew in, so Valerie tore through them, slamming each into the next. Stabbing one, then using it at the end of her sword like a baseball bat to slam a worker bot into the air so that it exploded against another drone. As she plowed through them with the others fighting behind her, one hit her with an explosive that blew her through a wall into the chamber behind them.

She stood up in a rage, eyes glowing bright red, and tore into them until it was just her crouching there, breathing heavily, and Robin and Lolack staring at her in awe.

"Damn fine work," Lolack said with a nod. "Keep it up."

He led the charge through the newly-discovered passage, leaping to the next level of the metal shelves. They were running now, jumping and throwing themselves from ledge to ledge, and as a red light would turn to green they would duck into a new area before Aranaught had time to process where they were.

The AI shouted in frustration and a hail of bullets fell upon the area, pinging off metal and causing several small explosions. When it was over, Lolack turned and smiled.

"Shooting randomly," he said. "This AI can't see us."

"And our friends?"

Lolack motioned them over. From beside him they could see the sky above, drones moving past, and the silver edge of something. The *Grandeur*!

Valerie lunged forward, but Lolack held out a hand to stop her. If she'd wanted to keep moving that hand wouldn't have done a damn thing, but she held back.

"We can't just charge out there," he said.

"Why not?" Robin asked.

Valerie glanced around, about to laugh, but then thought, *Yeah, why not?* She turned back to Lolack.

He pondered it, watching the drones, then said, "Actually you might be right. If the AI doesn't have complete control—if it hasn't taken over your ship and parked it there—it might be that the main AI hub isn't close enough. We charge out, 'we' meaning you two, and get that ship going. If you can do a manual override and it doesn't have the power to shut you down, you might have a shot at this."

"And you?" Valerie asked.

"I run to it as soon as the door's opened," he replied.

Valerie shook her head. "You're too valuable to us. I go and get her ready, and the two of you follow."

Lolack turned to Robin, who nodded.

"There you go," Valerie said, pleased with herself, and turned back to prepare the assault. As she took her first step, a barrage of fire rang out and she heard Garcia shouting.

"Val! *GET THE FUCK IN HERE!*"

"Scrap all of that, they're there!" Valerie said. "*Move!*"

As one, the three of them charged toward the ship. Valerie used her sword and pistol to cut into bots and shoot drones while Robin blasted through them with her rifle.

Lolack had to stay low, considering how tall he was, but he charged behind them with the courage of the admiral he was.

Bullets hit the ledge next to Valerie's head and she ducked, then saw that they had come from Garcia.

"Oh, damn!" he shouted, waving her over and redirecting his fire. "Get over here! Flynn took the ship back!"

Flynn was at the door, fidgeting with something at the side, while Arlay and Garcia shot down drones and worker bots.

"You didn't tell me you had a hacker on board!" Lolack said. "That changes everything!"

"How so?" Valerie shouted, pulling back to hold him against the closest wall as drone shots came at them.

"Get me and him together close to the AI hub, we might be able to put a stop to this nonsense."

"Great! You just increased your value to this mission about a thousandfold."

He grinned. "You have no idea what I'm capable of, but I promise to keep bringing the surprises if you keep it exciting."

She frowned and returned fire, then nodded for him to follow her as she led the charge to the next spot of cover behind several large metal crates that resembled refrigerators.

When they had crouched again she asked, "Why'd you leave, exactly?"

"Let's just say that I forgot what I was fighting for."

She frowned, but his gaze was directed past her to the doorway from which Garcia and Arlay were firing into the enemy ranks. That wasn't just a curious or focused stare either, but one of excitement and passion. He had agreed to come with them at the mention of Arlay, but Valerie had figured it was something military-related.

To her surprise, he was suddenly charging right through it all. Arlay saw him and charged too, leaping to knock him out of the way before a shot hit him, and then the two stood clasped in each other's arms as the fighting went on around them. Mostly that meant Valerie held off the enemy as she shouted at them to get the hell into the ship.

Arlay heard her first, helping him up and holding his arm tightly as they ran. She used the gun in her free hand to shoot at the enemy. Valerie followed them into the ship and Robin was the last, shooting down more drones and scanning the air for more before following them in. The whole scrapyard was ablaze, half-functional robots trying to get to them and Aranaught shouting that she was going to rip Valerie and her ship in half, but then the door was closed and they flew out of there.

"How the hell did you do that?" Valerie asked Flynn, who still stood at the door with a screen plugged into a section of the wall he'd torn open.

"We're overriding some of the ship's typical—"

"Okay, I wasn't asking about the details," she interrupted, glad to see them leaving it all behind. "I meant...wow."

He beamed.

"You think you can hold onto control when we're closer to Aranaught?" Robin asked.

Flynn looked doubtful.

"He can, with my help," Lolack said, his arm still wrapped around Arlay.

"So... This is a thing?" Valerie asked.

Arlay nodded, looking curiously at Lolack. "I thought it was in the past. Forgotten."

"I said that, I know..." Lolack glanced around, clearly

wishing the two were alone. On a ship this size though, that couldn't happen easily. "Listen, I lost track of myself, but no more. What's worth fighting for if you don't fight for yourself and ones you love?"

She leaned in to him, smiling and pressing her smooth blue skin against his deep orange. It was an odd image but Valerie smiled, trying to ignore that part of it.

The ship was turning toward the sky when Lolack pulled himself away and shouted, "Wait!"

"What is it?" Garcia asked, from the pilot seat.

"We can't go yet," Lolack said, "not until I pass on what I've learned to the locals. They'll need it. With the drop-pings of the sand snakes they will be able to farm and not rely on the stones, meaning no more war. I must do this."

Of course they agreed, and soon were flying back toward Wokana and her people. They would pass it on and trust them to spread the news.

CHAPTER TWENTY

"I wish Lolack were here," Mej said as they approached the meeting ground, an isolated island miles away from the Lavkin ships.

"We all do," Lien replied, "but we have faith in you and your ability to handle this, as did he. That was the reason he left you in charge."

"Yes," Mej said doubtfully, as if trying to convince herself.

Jilla watched them both as the small boat they were on neared the island. It was just the three of them, though air support was circling high overhead. They'd made the decision as a group that it probably wouldn't be a good idea to bring a Bandian to a meeting with the Wandarby cultists, although Jilla personally thought it would be pretty funny.

They'd decided Jilla should come along instead, to see how they reacted to a Pallicon on the enemy side.

The boat reached the shore, and Jilla hopped out and dragged it onto the beach. Mej and Lien stepped out onto dry land, and they approached the three enemy representatives.

All three of the Pallicons were dressed in the black robes of Wandarby priests. They looked almost comical standing there in their heavy garb, their arms folded into the sleeves as they waited in the hot midday sun. Their eyes widened when they saw Jilla, but none of them said anything.

Mej waited until they were about four feet away before speaking. "You wanted to meet?"

The priest in the middle nodded slightly. "We are aware one of our temple warships has been attacking you for the past several months."

"We noticed that too," Mej said drily.

"For this, I would like to apologize on behalf of the entirety of the Wandarby Church. They should have attempted to speak peacefully, as we are doing now, before escalating things."

"Apology excepted. I appreciate you coming all this way. Enjoy your journey home."

The priest held up a hand. "We are not finished. What the local temple *should* have done was to make the simple offer we make now: hand over every Bandian hiding in your ships, and allow us to search them to ensure you have overlooked none. We will then station soldiers on your ships for the next two solar cycles. As penance for housing members of an evil race who threatens the entire galaxy, you will donate one-tenth of all your possessions to the Wandarby Church. Are these terms acceptable?"

The corners of Mej's mouth raised in a tiny smile. "Not remotely."

The priest's expression was unreadable. "Are you aware of the Bandians' destiny? By continuing to aid them, you show yourself to be an enemy of life itself. The galaxy is a flower in a fist that prepares to—"

"Let me stop you there," Jilla said, unable to help herself. "I've heard this sermon before, and it gets really boring."

For the first time since he'd started speaking, the priest's expression changed. His nose scrunched up in disgust. "You are a shame to your people."

Even though this guy was an idiot cultist, that stung a little. She'd grown up around a wild mix of species on SEDE, and she'd never felt like a true member of Pallicon society. She'd always been an outsider, but instead of being used to it, that only made it hurt worse. "Maybe my people are a shame to *me*. This group of them, anyway."

Mej held up a hand, silencing her. "I have a counteroffer for you. Leave now, and we won't follow you. We'll forget this ever happened."

"I don't think so," the priest replied. "We outnumber you five to one. Your ships have been converted into boats, so they can't even fly to defend you. What do you have?"

"We have a Pallicon named Irem." She let that hang in the air for a moment. "He told us you'd ask for this little meetup. He also told us it was a distraction so you could flank us."

"Irem's a traitor and a fool," the priest growled.

"Maybe, but he was right about this meeting. He said you had no intention of negotiating a real peace."

"Then why'd you come?" the priest asked.

"You wanted time to get your people in position," she said with a smile. "So did we."

Kalan surged toward the Wandarby squadron in the stolen Pallicon fighter. It appeared they hadn't been ready for the fight to begin, and now they were scrambling—just as Kalan had hoped.

"I bet these guys weren't expecting us to bring the fight to them," one of the other pilots said in Kalan's headset.

"That's life," Kalan replied. "You don't always get what you expect."

Up ahead, he spotted a squadron of fighters so thick it might have been a dark cloud. Clearly there was no order to their formation. The Wandarby cult had the numbers and the technology, but when it came to military discipline they made a piss-poor showing.

He picked a target near the center of the cloud of ships and fired. As the smoke rose from the fighter, he let out an involuntary, "Yeah!"

All around him, the Lavkin fighters were laying into their Wandarby counterparts, picking them off and then ducking out of range. He had to admit the Lavkins were insanely accomplished flyers. It was a risky move, putting their fighters on the offensive rather than keeping them down where they could protect the ships, but he had felt like it would be worth it, and so had Mej. If they could keep the Wandarby off balance long enough, they might be able survive until the other part of Kalan's plan came through.

He fired again, tagging another of the Wandarby craft in the left wing. The enemy fighter careened wildly, spiraling downward when its pilot lost control.

Then he saw it. The ship hovered a little west of the disorganized cloud of fighters. It looked exactly as Irem had described it, so he recognized it immediately: the High Priest's ship.

It was smaller than a warship, and larger than a fighter. According to Irem, the most important dozen or so priests would be aboard that ship. The priests served as military leaders as well as spiritual ones, so if they could take down that ship they'd put a sizable hole in the Wandarby command.

Thankfully the ship had descended into Rewot's atmosphere, so all they had to do was bring it down.

"I've got eyes on the High Priest's ship," he said into his headset.

"Roger that," the lead pilot said. "I got it too. All fighters, target that ship."

"They're going to protect it with everything they've got," Kalan pointed out.

"Then we'd better take it down fast."

Kalan smiled. As hesitant as these Lavkins could be in hand-to-hand combat, it was surprising how bold they were in the skies. It was a true pleasure to fly with them.

He banked hard to the west and raced toward the ship. The cloud of fighters near it still seemed to be wildly disorganized. Their troops were already on the ground, Kalan knew, and they were likely having a tough time getting their priorities straight. Go after the Lavkin fighters, or support their troops on the ground?

Either way, the chaos wouldn't last long. Kalan knew they had to take advantage of this moment.

Five Lavkin fighters beat Kalan to the High Priest's

ship, and they wasted no time in attempting to take it down. They hit it with a massive barrage of firepower, even while barrel-rolling and constantly shifting position to avoid the ship's railguns.

Seeing his allies performing so well only motivated Kalan to make sure he didn't miss out on the action. He spotted a Pallicon fighter at three o'clock and turned hard, shooting it down before it knew he was there, and went around to the other side of the High Priest's ship.

Then he locked onto the ship and unleashed everything he had.

"It's going down!" the squad leader shouted.

"Oh, hell yeah!" Kalan exclaimed as the High Priest's damaged ship succumbed to gravity and tumbled toward the sea.

"This isn't over yet," the squad leader reminded them. "All we've done so far is piss them off. Let's take care of those fighters."

As the others in his squad set about doing just that, Kalan broke off from the group and pointed the nose of his ship downward. He had other orders to follow. The plan he'd worked out with Mej, Lien, and the others before the battle was playing out perfectly so far, so it was time to move on to the next step.

Just because the High Priest's ship was going down didn't mean Kalan was finished with it.

Bob stood on top of *Flamebird* with the detonator in his hand. As soon as Commander Larence gave him the signal he'd press the button.

"Ask the commander what we're waiting for," Wearl said, her voice thick with impatience.

"He already told us," Bob replied. "We want to let as many of them get on the walkways as possible."

As Mej had anticipated the Pallicons had made their initial landing on the island, unloading three transports' worth of troops. The Lavkins had put up a minor show of defending the central location, but they'd quickly fallen back.

The troops from the first transport were on the network of metal walkways between the ships now, but the second and third waves were still waiting for their chance to get in on the action. The Lavkin soldiers were taking shots at the approaching enemies from the top of *Flamebird*, not so much to take them out as because it would have looked suspicious if they hadn't.

Commander Larence sidled up next to Bob. "The soldiers from the second wave are almost all on the walkways. If we wait much longer, we'll have too many on this side. Do it."

Bob grinned. "All right. Take this, you shapeshifting bastards." He pressed the button.

A cascade of *booms* rang out as the explosives planted beneath the walkways went off in quick succession.

Pallicon soldiers flew into the air, blown clear of the walkway, but more importantly, they'd destroyed the only things connecting the island and the ships. The soldiers on the island were stranded; any troops who wanted to get to the ships now would either have to do it through the air or swim for it.

A cheer went up among those gathered on the top of *Flamebird*, but Commander Larence whirled on them. "We'll celebrate when the battle's over. For now, concentrate on the enemies trying to board our damn ship."

Larence was right. While most of the Pallicon troops were stranded on the island, a couple dozen remained on this side too. These had no choice but to attack.

"Waiting's over, Wearl," Bob said, drawing his weapon. He wished he had the giant rifle he'd taken from the mech on the moon of Tol, but that was still on the *Grandeur*. The Lavkin carbine in his hands would have to do.

"Way ahead of you," she said, and her Shimmer-designed rifle *boomed*. A Pallicon climbing the side of the ship fell backwards into the water with a hole in his chest.

"Starboard side!" Commander Larence called.

Bob dashed to the starboard side of the ship in time to see ten Pallicons reach the top. He fired at the closest, hitting him in the forehead and sending him reeling over the edge.

One of them rushed forward and grabbed his arm, and Bob cried out as the creature's fingers dug in. The Pallicon raised his weapon but Bob was faster, firing point blank and dropping the enemy soldier.

He saw movement out of the corner of his left eye and spun toward it. Commander Larence rushed up to him, a look of urgency on his face. Bob paused to see what he'd say, but the commander simply stared at him. He had a gun in his hand, and he was raising it.

Over Commander Larence's shoulder, Bob saw something that made him gasp—another Commander Larence, this one engaged in a fight with another group of Pallicons. Wandarby weren't allowed to use their shapeshifting abilities until they'd killed a Lavkin or a Bandian. Once they had, all bets were off.

That guy fighting the Pallicons had to be the real Commander Larence, which meant…

He shot the false Commander Larence, and the Pallicon shifted back to his true form as he died.

"Nice work!" Commander Larence called across the deck. "Everyone, stay alert like Bob. Our enemies can shift their appearance."

"Yeah," Bob said with a smile. "Be like me." He had to admit, it felt pretty good.

CHAPTER TWENTY-ONE

Wokana and her Lavkins were overjoyed at the news, promising to share the word with their kin in the moving city. It made sense to do so, since that would mean no more war. They invited Valerie and her team to stay for a celebratory meal, but the enemy now knew where they were. They needed to get out as soon as possible so as not to put these innocents at risk.

They were moving out to the *Grandeur*, a line of Lavkins trailing behind and saying farewell with the head bowing, when another signal sounded from the ship. Flynn, who had gone back early to check for trouble, appeared at the doorway.

"We have a communication from Jilla and Wearl," he said. "Looks like they have information for us."

Valerie and the others quickly said their farewells, making for the ship to see what was going on. Flynn pulled up the message, and there was Jilla on the screen.

"They sent it while the ship was disabled," Flynn explained, then hit play.

"Valerie and all members of the *Grandeur*," Jilla said. "If you get this, we have important information. The AI known as Aranaught has infiltrated many corners of this side of the galaxy, but we have one specific piece of intel. Aranaught has located Admiral Lolack's second-in-command, Captain Tenowk, and is sending a sizeable force to take him out. The good news? You are close enough that if you get this message, you might be able to get there first. We hope you've gotten it in time, and will keep trying to reach you."

With that the communication ended, replaced by coordinates that went straight into the system.

"Proceed?" Flynn asked.

Valerie breathed deeply as she turned to Lolack and said, "Sounds like we don't have a choice."

"Thank you," Lolack replied.

"Flynn or Garcia?" Valerie frowned. "Flynn, you're the better pilot now, right?"

Flynn nodded. "But I've been training Garcia just in case."

"Smart thinking, but for now, get us to those coordinates as fast as possible. Everyone else, I know we haven't had much time to catch our breath, but we're off the grid now, meaning that son of a bitch AI won't be able to take us over or shut down our power." She glanced at Lolack, who nodded his confirmation. "We're going to teach him not to mess with Lolack or any members of the Lost Fleet —er, sorry, *Lolack's* Fleet."

"Hell yeah!" Garcia said, followed by an "Oorah."

"I like this one," Lolack said, towering over Garcia as he clapped him on the shoulder.

Soon they were en route to kick some AI cyber-ass, but Arlay looked especially nervous. It couldn't be about the upcoming fight, Valerie thought, so she leaned in and asked how she was doing.

Arlay nodded to the back and stood, so Valerie went with her. When they were out of earshot of the rest Arlay sighed and glanced around, then went into it.

"When I mentioned before that many of my people have become pirates..." Arlay glanced up at Valerie. "It's the reason Admiral Lolack's family didn't approve of us being together."

"Wait, what?" Valerie leaned forward. "Why is this the first time I'm hearing of this? You two were a couple?"

"No, we weren't. We loved each other, but his parents wouldn't hear of it. He tried to throw it all away for me, but I wouldn't let him. I refused. I know this is very egocentric, but...when you mentioned before that Lolack left because he felt he'd lost track of what he was fighting for, I can't help wonder..."

"If that something was you?" Valerie assessed her, impressed. "Wow! You know, that makes sense. How's it feel to be responsible for the dissolution of the Lost Fleet?"

"Ugh, don't say that!" Arlay would have blushed if she could have.

"Oh my God," Valerie stood and took her hand. "I'm so sorry. I was totally not being serious. But...wow. I mean it, I'm sorry."

"But you agree that it might have been all my fault?"

Valerie scrunched her nose in thought. She'd heard of men doing much worse for love. "Well, now it's up to you, isn't it?"

"How so?"

"You two get a second chance, and it doesn't look like he's going to let his parents' thoughts about it get in the way this time. Neither should you."

"But his reputation—"

"Will be fine." Valerie turned so she too could see Lolack, where he and Flynn were nerd-talking about hacking and how to take on the AI. "Think about it— without knowing you were there for him, he left the fleet behind. He only turned to our side back there when we mentioned your name. He needs you, Arlay, meaning the universe needs the two of you to be together."

"Now that's some pressure!" Arlay said with a laugh.

"Pressure toward what you both want anyway. Let it push aside any worries you have about his parents."

Arlay nodded and thanked Valerie, then walked over to join Lolack and Flynn.

"Look at you," Garcia said, returning from the restroom. "While you're giving relationship advice, maybe you can help me?"

"Shut up."

He laughed. "I'm serious! See..." He held up his right hand, then his left, looking from one to the other. "Mr. Righty here was my sole lover until lately, and he's getting a tad jealous of Mr. Lefty, so—"

"Disgusting," Valerie said, walking away to the sound of Garcia's laughter.

"Help me, Val!" he called after her. "I don't know what to do!"

"What was that about?" Robin asked, glancing at Garcia as Valerie took the nearby seat.

"Garcia being a *man*."

"Oh, that's what Mr— Yeah, got it." Robin laughed. "Well, at least he can use those hands to kill enemies too. We're about to need them."

"Can we talk about something other than his hands?" Valerie asked. "I don't need that image in my mind. Dammit, too late. Ugh…"

"Just throw yourself in there too, and at least—"

"Stop!" Valerie reached out and hit Robin in the shoulder hard. "Not funny!"

Robin kept laughing and rubbed her shoulder. "Come on now, Garcia certainly isn't bad looking. Even if you don't want to get serious, you could have worse fantasies."

Valerie laid back and closed her eyes, but couldn't get the image out of her mind. "I'm going."

"Where?"

"Away from all of you, that's for damn sure." She stood and went to join the hackers in their nerd talk, figuring she would absorb whatever she could just in case. They'd be there soon, and she wanted to be focused.

CHAPTER TWENTY-TWO

Kalan piloted his fighter toward the spot he'd seen the High Priest's ship go down. It wasn't difficult to find; as soon as he broke through the clouds, he saw a giant splash.

"Ha! Got you, bastards!" he muttered.

He circled a few times, giving the water a chance to calm down a little, then set his fighter down in the water. This was the all-in moment. His stolen ship wasn't built to float, so he wouldn't be lifting off again. That was fine with him. Either he'd be dead soon, or he'd have the High Priest. Either way, he wouldn't need this fighter again.

Kalan popped open the cockpit and jumped into the cool, salty water. The High Priest's ship sent tendrils of smoke curling into the sky as Kalan swam toward it, using long, powerful strokes to cover the fifty yards quickly.

The ship was floating on top of the water for now, but Kalan knew that wouldn't last. As seawater seeped into the fractured hull, it would eventually sink. Kalan hoped he could get to the High Priest before that happened.

Finding his way into the ship was easy. He just held

onto the hull near the largest airlock he could find. Sure enough, it was only a few moments before a panicked survivor threw it open. Kalan shot the male Pallicon with his Tralen-14, then climbed inside.

The interior of the ship was dim, lit only by the emergency lights. Kalan didn't know the layout of the ship, but he didn't need to. He followed the angry shouts down the corridor in front of him.

The ship wasn't large—it was significantly smaller than the *Grandeur*—but it had landed in the water at an odd angle, Navigating the tilted hallway took longer than Kalan would have liked. When he reached the end, he paused and listened.

"Respectfully, Your Holiness, don't you think we should abandon ship?" a timid voice asked.

"What a brilliant idea!" came the sarcastic response. "Let's jump out of our floating vessel and tread water in this alien sea that's probably filled with deadly creatures we've never even heard of."

"But Your Holiness," another voice pled, "we won't be floating forever. We will sink."

"I am the High Priest of the Wandarby Church, the one true church of the Pallicon people. My army will *not* let me drown!"

That was all Kalan needed to hear. It sounded like he'd found the right place. He burst through the door, his Tralen-14 held at the ready.

Four figures stood in the middle of the room. One of them was dressed in the blackest robe Kalan had ever seen, and he took a big step back as Kalan entered. That would be the High Priest. Kalan would save him for last.

The other three Pallicon males stepped forward. Whether they were guards, less important priests, or simply the crew of the ship, Kalan didn't know. But they were between him and his target, and that meant their crazy cultist lives were about to come to an end.

He quickly squeezed off a round, dropping the guard on the left. The one in the center froze, and Kalan took him out just as easily. The third one was smarter. He drew his weapon and took careful aim while Kalan dispatched his two buddies.

Kalan saw the emergency lights glittering off the Pallicon's weapon and lunged backward, causing the shot to miss. Then he crouched and charged.

He hit the Pallicon hard and wrapped his arms around him, tackling him to the deck. Keeping one knee on the male's chest, he drew his pistol and fired.

Now it was just Kalan and the High Priest.

The High Priest raised a tiny pistol and pointed it at Kalan with a shaky hand.

Kalan snarled and sprang to his feet, and the priest let out a high-pitched squeal of fear. Kalan plucked the pistol from the priest's hand and hit him in the face with it, and the priest landed on his back on the deck.

"So you're the guy, huh?" Kalan stalked toward him as he spoke. "You're the one who runs this cult? The cult that killed my people?"

A defiant look appeared on the priest's face. "Killed? More like exterminated. It was no more than you evil vermin deserved."

Kalan crouched next to him. "How many Bandians have you killed?"

The priest looked away. "In truth, you're the first one I've met."

Kalan laughed. "I'm sorry, but that's hilarious. You spent your whole life looking for a Bandian, and the one you find ends up killing you? Kind of ironic."

"I'll die gladly if I know you go down with me."

Kalan ignored the comment. It didn't deserve a response. "Here's what I need. I need to address the entire Wandarby army at once. Can you make that happen?"

Now the priest chuckled. "Of course I could, but am I going to? For you? Never."

"Wanna make a bet?"

Five minutes and a few broken cult-leader bones later, Kalan had located the comm system and had it properly tuned to address the entire Wandarby army. He took a deep breath and began to speak.

"Greetings, Wandarby true believers. My name is Kalan Grayhewn, and I'm the Bandian you are so violently looking for." He paused a moment to let them take that in. He imagined it would be strange for them to hear their enemy in their ears, and he didn't want them to miss his next words.

"You think my kind are the scourge of the galaxy," he continued. "You think there are a whole bunch of Bandians hidden in this Lavkin squadron. You think your fight is against my Bandian family, but actually it's against something much worse. See, I don't *have* a Bandian family. Other than my mother, I don't know another living Bandian. But I have something that is much worse for you. I have the family I fight beside every day."

He walked to where the High Priest was sitting on the ground, listening in horror.

"I have my newest family members, the Lavkins—the ones kicking your asses right now. I have my crewmates—a strange collection of humans, a Shimmer, and a Pallicon. Then there's my boss, the Prime Enforcer. Trust me when I say you do not want to be here when she gets back. You'd be better off fighting a whole battalion of Bandians than facing her when she's angry."

He paused for a moment, wondering what Valerie would think of this situation. She probably would have ripped off the High Priest's head by now.

"I have some other friends too, whom you'll be meeting soon. I don't want to ruin the surprise. My point is this: the Wandarby cult is done. If you are lucky enough to be one of the few Pallicons who survives this battle, I highly suggest you buy a ticket for the farthest planet you can afford to get to, and when you arrive you start a peaceful new life. Because I am going to make it my mission to hunt down each and every Pallicon who dares call him or herself a Wandarby. I'm going to hunt you like you hunted my kind. And if there are any other Bandians living out there somewhere in this galaxy, I'm going to make damn sure they don't have to worry about being your next victims."

He raised his gun.

"And I'm going to start with your High Priest."

The Pallicon had just enough time to open his mouth before Kalan squeezed the trigger.

"You think Bandians are evil? Dangerous? Something to

feared? You have no idea. Wandarby, it's time for you to start running."

With that, he dropped the radio and headed for the airlock. The ship and the High Priest's body would soon be at the bottom of the sea where they belonged.

When Jilla climbed aboard *Flamebird*, she was shocked at the number of Pallicons and the ferocity with which the Lavkins were fighting them. Though they were greatly outnumbered, the Lavkins showed no fear.

So far during the battle Jilla had traveled from ship to ship with Mej and Lien, helping to assess the situation on each and making strategic adjustments on the fly. Now they were on Lien's ancestral ship, where the fighting was the heaviest.

Bob dashed over as he spotted her. "You okay?"

She nodded. "Where can I help?"

"The starboard side is where we're having the most trouble."

"Bob!" one of the Lavkins called. "We need your help over here! They're slamming us."

Bob grinned at Jilla. "Also, I'm basically a war hero now." He turned and ran to the guy who'd called him.

"Transport!" someone shouted.

Jilla looked up and saw a transport ship racing through the sky toward them. It hovered fifteen feet above *Flamebird* and opened its cargo door, and twenty Wandarby cultists leaped out. Jilla knew from experience that a fifteen-foot drop was no big deal for a Pallicon.

She found some cover on the starboard side of the ship and started firing at the new arrivals.

Suddenly something changed. One moment, the Pallicons were in full assault mode, and the next they had their hands over their earpieces, listening.

"The Bandian!" one of them shouted. "How dare he!"

Jilla smiled. She didn't know exactly what Kalan was up to, but whatever it was seemed to be throwing off the Wandarby, and she was going to take advantage of that.

She took out three of them as they listened dumbly to the voice on their headsets.

"Nice shot," a male voice next to her said.

She turned and saw Commander Larence crouching next to her. "Thanks. We've got a long way to go, though." She glanced up at the transport disappearing into the sky. She didn't want to say it aloud, but they were in trouble. As valiantly as they were fighting, at a certain point it came down to numbers. If the Wandarby really had thousands of soldiers to throw at the Lavkins, eventually the Lavkins would lose."

Commander Larence squinted at something across the ship. "What the hell is he doing over there?" Then, more loudly, "Kalan! We're over here!"

Jilla saw it was indeed Kalan rushing across the deck toward them. Larence raised himself into a near-standing position and waved his arms so Kalan could spot them.

As the figure drew closer, Jilla saw the edge of 'Kalan's' shoulder flicker. "Commander, that's not—"

The false Kalan brought up a Pallicon weapon and fired, shooting Commander Larence directly in the face.

"No!" Jilla shouted. She squeezed three quick rounds

into the false Kalan's chest and he fell, returning to his Pallicon form. But the damage had been done. Commander Larence was dead.

She barely had time to shut the Lavkin's eyes before she heard the dreaded cry once again. "Transport!"

"Holy hell," she muttered. "Will they ever run out of these guys?"

She wished the real Kalan were here. Not that he'd be able to save them from these insane odds, but it sure would be nice to have him by her side if this really was the end.

She squeezed off another round, dropping a Pallicon who'd been dumb enough to stick his head into the open. Still, they'd only managed to take out about half the last group of Wandarby, and now another group was leaping out of their transport.

Mej and Lien were crouching behind a metal barricade not far away, and she scurried over to them.

"What are you two still doing here?" she asked. "You need to get somewhere safe."

Mej shook her head and raised her weapon. "This is where the fighting is heaviest, so this is where we belong."

"Besides," Lien added, "this is my family's ship. There's no way I can leave it."

Jilla grimaced. From the determination on their faces, it was clear they'd be no talking them out of staying here until the bitter end. "Hey, I want to say that what you guys did—welcoming us into your family—it meant a lot to us, and especially to Kalan. He wants a family more than anything, so that was just about the best gift he could ever receive."

Lien nodded. "It was our pleasure, but don't talk like this is the end. We're going to get through this."

"Yeah? You got a secret plan I don't know about?"

"No," Mej said, looking past Jilla and toward the sky, "but maybe they can help."

Jilla followed her gaze and gasped. Dozens of massive round ships decorated with strange red lettering were firing on the Wandarby.

She knew whose ships those were. She'd seen ships like that around SEDE on a daily basis.

The Shimmer Fleet had arrived, and they were fighting for the Lavkins.

CHAPTER TWENTY-THREE

The journey to find Captain Tenowk had been an easy one. It was the battle on planet that was going to be the challenge. As they approached the location—what had once been a destination planet, a paradise to which Tenowk had apparently come to spend the rest of his days with beautiful vibrantly-yellow-skinned women—it was clear Aranaught had taken over.

Flynn highlighted the security system on the display, emphasizing the land-based surface-to-outer-atmosphere missiles, well-equipped cruisers, and what translated from Lavkin as a Juggernaut-class destroyer.

"Maybe we should reach out to Nathan Lowell," Robin suggested. "This might be over our heads."

"Except that as we've seen in the past, Aranaught suffers from an excess of hubris," Arlay countered.

Lolack stood beside Valerie's seat, tall and in charge as if this were his ship. It was only slightly annoying.

"If Flynn's as good as I think he is," the admiral said, "he'll pull it off. Continue as planned."

"Sir?" Flynn asked, glancing back from the controls. "I can't outfly all that."

"Not outfly," the admiral said with a confident smile. "Your hacking skills. What do you think of not shutting down, but powering down to a minimal level and making those sensors out there think you're no more than a stray asteroid?"

"They wouldn't just let an asteroid in," Flynn argued, but then looked thoughtful. "Well, that would be true of the vacation hosts, but not necessarily of an AI that doesn't give two shits about the condition of the planet or the life thereon."

"Precisely," Lolack said. "And if they start to fire on us, we go to full engines and see how we do."

"Still the risk-taker," Arlay said, considering their options. "Even if the Etheric Federation has ships nearby that they can send, they would take a while to get here. It's not likely we'll have a chance of saving the captain by that point.

"And since that's what we're here to do," Lolack said, "that isn't an option."

"Try the rock idea," Valerie said, shaking her head at the thought of it. "What do we have to lose? Other than our lives and this war, of course."

"Ignoring sarcasm and following orders," Flynn replied, turning the controls over to Garcia and making for one of the computer screens that he and Lolack had set up for situations like this.

"You sure you can do this?" Valerie asked.

"It's a simple matter of intercepting their comm, replacing any messaging they have to process our arrival, and then putting our own message in." Flynn waved off the question. "Piece of cake. At least, I hope it will be."

"Coming in hot," Arlay said. "Now or never."

Lolack nodded his approval of Valerie's decision to give it a go and went over to help Flynn. The joy of space is that it's humongous. While scanners could easily pick them up from afar, if one went undetected slipping in without being spotted by eye or running across enemy ships was easy.

Once they passed the first lines of what their system had warned was the outer defense they all sat up a little straighter, waiting for alarms, warnings, or any sort of attack. Nothing.

"Everything's going according to plan," Flynn said, voice hushed.

"Keep it up," Valerie replied, watching the planet grow larger as they entered atmosphere. Soon they were barreling toward the resort section of the planet.

There was no question that Aranaught was here. A carpet of mechs covered the resort's beach. There were humanoids around too, but Valerie sensed they weren't the normal resort types. Judging by the glints off their skin from the sun, they were cyborgs.

Then there was a shift, as if everything on that beach noticed their approach at once.

"Prepare yourselves," Valerie shouted. The mechs had begun to move, lifting into the sky to intercept them. "Do we have to worry about the destroyer? The turrets?"

"We're too close for all that now," Lolack said, "so stay that way. Flynn, get back to the controls. I got it from here."

"I'll be on weapons," Garcia said, returning to his seat to prepare to blow the enemy out of the sky.

"Good, keep them busy," Valerie replied. "Just get me on the ground so I can find this guy and get him out of there."

"The fuck!" Robin turned to her, pissed. "You're not going down there until we know it's safe!"

"Watch me."

Robin took a breath and shook her head. "Not without me."

"And me," Lolack added.

"You're too important to the mission," Valerie protested.

"I know, but you need Flynn up here to fly and ensure the ship doesn't fall into Aranaught's hands. Down there you need someone Tenowk recognizes, and you need that someone to be able to find the AI hub and end this."

"He has a point," Arlay said, though her voice showed she clearly hated the idea.

"We have a short window on that," Flynn said, "so make a final decision, because I'm doing a low pass right now."

"Now?" Valerie asked, standing up and looking for her helmet as she did her best to balance herself.

"*NOW!*" he shouted, as they came in fast and close to the resort. He pointed to the back doors and said, "Opening now. You're going to want chutes just to break the fall, but cut them loose if they drag you back."

"Lolack," Valerie turned to him, nervous, "stay behind us as much as possible. And...keep low."

He laughed, reaching for the equipment he'd picked up on the space station—bought from the pirates—and suited up while Arlay fetched them chutes and helped Lolack strap his on. She finished with a gentle kiss.

"Come back, or this time I'll come after you myself," she threatened.

"Nothing could keep me from you now," he replied. "That's a promise."

"*SHUT UP AND GO!*" Flynn yelled and Valerie and Robin headed toward the rear of the ship, pulling Lolack with them.

A moment later they leaped out the back, their chutes blossoming and yanking them hard, then they hit the packed sand of the jungle outside the resort. Valerie cut the straps off in an instant, then moved at vampire speed to Robin and then Lolack, helping to free them.

Thump. Thump. Thump.

The ground shook around them and two seconds later a large mech ran at them, blue shield up and rockets at the ready.

"Mine," Robin shouted, darting right in a flash.

"Mechs versus vampires," Valerie said with a smile. "This should be fun." She shouted a warning to Lolack, then sprinted in the direction opposite Robin. The mech was already confused. It fired after Robin first, but a moment later she used her strength to twist its shoulder mount so that the next shots exploded in the barrel. The mech stood still and dissolved the shield, preparing to fire its launchers at her, but she was gone and then Valerie hit from the other side, using her super-strength to take out one of its legs. It was too heavy even for her but she was able to knock it off balance, and it fell over and landed like a turtle.

They opened up on it until they hit its energy core, and Robin yelled, "Back!"

They returned to Lolack's side, holding him down as the mech exploded and took down two more that were about to join the fight.

"There you are!" Aranaught's voice came out loud and clear from the resort. "But you're too late. He's already mine."

"Not a chance," Lolack said, charging forward.

A wave of cyborgs met them, while the *Grandeur* shot another mech out of the sky and turned on the rest that were converging on Valerie's location.

"We need to get inside fast," Valerie said, shooting down the two closest cyborgs.

"I can run," Lolack replied. "These legs are long for a reason."

She glanced at him and nodded. "Go. I'll cover the two of you, then join you."

They took off while she mowed down more of the cyborgs. One scaled a tree with his metal arms and threw himself at her, but she drew her sword and sidestepped to cleave him in two. Two more came bounding in on metal legs, but they met fire from Robin. A glance showed Lolack hadn't been exaggerating; he was damn fast. Not vampire-fast, but close enough.

"Get over here!" Robin shouted, sending a barrage of bullets into the jungle where the cyborgs were coming from.

Valerie ran to her and they darted around the back of the resort building, crashing in through a window and plowing down two more cyborgs that had been waiting for them.

Another figure moved at the top of the stairs and Valerie spun to shoot, but Lolack knocked her rifle aside.

"No, that's him!" Lolack gestured to the male Valerie could now see was tall, with vibrant orange skin under his red robes—only he clearly wasn't himself. Half his face was metal, and there was glass covering one eye. "Or mostly him."

"You should shoot me," Tenowk said, descending the stairs one at a time while the sounds of chaos and explosions continued outside. Then his voice took on a more feminine robotic tone. "As I said, your friend is mine."

Aranaught had him.

Valerie considered lifting her rifle to shoot, but Lolack was still standing in the way, hand held out.

"You're still in there, brother. I know you too well." Lolack took a step forward to meet his brother-in-arms and dearest friend. "I see you before me, and I'm not leaving here without you. That's a promise."

The *Grandeur* made a pass, followed by the building shaking and more explosions nearby.

"Dammit, don't take us out too!" Robin shouted into her comm.

"I'm not sure how you've kept the ship from me," Aranaught said, "but I'll have it soon enough. Trust me, you can't win this."

"You're a machine," Valerie replied. "How could a machine have any concept of what we're capable of?"

Tenowk growled and lifted his hands, and Valerie saw that while he had no weapons, the ship that Aranaught had been housed in had re-formed itself into an internal defensive system. There were weapons on all sides of them. Advanced, but also foolish.

It meant this was the hub. They could take over Aranaught from here.

Her first move though, had to be to get Lolack out of harm's way. She leaped for him, grabbing him and rolling as the room lit up with gunfire.

"Take them out!" Valerie shouted to Robin, then took Lolack's arm and ran to the side hallway as more shots hit nearby. "It's here…the core!"

They reached cover, though the wall next to them was quickly shredding under a hail of bullets.

"But where?" he shouted over the noise, then motioned behind her. "Incoming!"

Sure enough, another mech plowed through the front entrance at that moment, a massive saw blade terminating one arm and what looked like a fifty-caliber machine gun the other.

Valerie was preparing to meet it when a thought hit her. Spinning around, she saw that it wasn't red robes on the man, but the metal on his face connected with more that ran down his back and bulged behind him.

"The fucker wanted us to survive this, to save your friend and bring him onto the ship." She processed this, shooting at the mech, and then broke after Lolack to get to cover.

"What do you mean?"

"I mean she knows how strong we are. This is all a ruse. If we take your friend aboard the *Grandeur* she'll be able to take over, and then we're hers."

"Or worse, she waits until we're at the fleet, then takes it *all* over."

Valerie cursed, checking her ammo and then quickly reloading. "But we can't leave him, so…"

"I need to work my magic, right?" He smiled. "Get me and him alone—that's all I need. Hold them off for two minutes. Can you do that?"

Valerie smiled and shrugged. "I don't see that we have any other choice."

The wall collapsed toward them and the ceiling starting to fall as the mech came in firing. Valerie sent Lolack one way while she charged in to take it down.

She had a plan now, and there would be no stopping her. She ran through the chaos, sabotaging mechs and taking down cyborgs on her way to Tenowk, trusting her guess that Aranaught was imbedded in him and therefore she wouldn't risk damaging the main part of her plan. When she reached him they went flying into the next room, and she shouted, "Lolack!"

"We have to escape," Tenowk said in his own voice, sounding desperate. "Get me out of here!"

All part of the ruse, she knew now.

She smiled and said, "Don't worry, we will." She threw him against one of the wall posts, and, hating herself for doing so, bent her sword around his neck to keep him in place.

"What…what are you doing?" he asked in panic. "They're here! They're going to kill us!"

"I don't think so," Lolack said, charging in and not wasting anytime. He tore off the robes, and found all manner of panels and other devices set up. "Two minutes!" he reminded Valerie.

"You got it," she replied, and then charged back out into the main room, rifle blazing. Robin was at her side in a flash, the two leapfrogging their attacks, and shouting into their comms for the *Grandeur* to keep enemies from entering the resort as much as possible.

Bullets rained down outside, and the fight continued.

As Valerie was smashing a cyborg's head to pieces, she heard Lolack calling for her.

"Keep them busy," she told Robin, then darted back up the stairs to find Lolack. Instead of finding the Lavkins finishing up on the technical side, she found Tenowk with a gun to the admiral's head, hand trembling.

"He's in there," Lolack said, smiling at his friend. "He knows me."

"We have to finish this!" Valerie shouted, ready to take this guy out.

"No," Lolack said, voice calm. "You have to finish it while I keep his attention."

"You can't defeat me," Aranaught said. "I'm everywhere! Trying to stomp me out of existence is like removing air. What would you do without air?"

"We're not removing you," Lolack answered, gesturing for Valerie to move to the back of Tenowk's head. The panel was open, and a series of wires there had been pulled free and reconnected in different ways. Only two still hung lose, metal exposed. When Lolack crossed his fingers, Valerie got the message. "Just...purifying you," he added, then motioned for her to act as he dodged left.

Tenowk's arm raised to shoot her, but Valerie was too

fast. She dashed forward, connecting the wires in a split-second, and then looked up to see if the shot hit. But it never came.

"Tell Flynn *now*!" Lolack commanded.

Valerie stared at him, confused, then at Tenowk.

"Do it!" Lolack said, and this time she reacted, repeating the word into her comm.

"Done," Flynn replied a moment later, and then there was silence.

No more explosions, no more shooting—just the thunder of the *Grandeur* and the remaining mechs landing outside.

"What exactly happened?" Valerie asked.

"We just purified Aranaught," Lolack said, grinning as he leaped up. "Tenowk, tell me it's you."

Tenowk's arm shook, and for a moment Valerie thought he was going to shoot. Instead, the gun fell to the floor and Tenowk strode forward to take Lolack in an odd embrace, arms bent with hands on each other's heads.

"It's me, old friend. And something more..." Tenowk felt the side of his face, the metal and the wiring. "Wh-what have they done to me?"

"What do you mean?"

Tenowk laughed. He actually laughed. "I paid for the deluxe spa package, but this wasn't on the menu."

Now Lolack laughed too, shaking his head as they stepped apart. "Brother, you're about to play a larger part in this war than you ever knew was possible."

"War?" Valerie asked.

Lolack turned to her, expression growing dark. "In my last struggle with Aranaught she revealed that, in her words, 'We are all doomed.' It seems she's put out signals to anyone who might be an enemy, calling them here to once and for all wipe the Lost Fleet from existence. Little do they know the Lost Fleet no longer exists—it is Lolack's Fleet again, and I mean to reunite it and stand against this enemy. More than that, I think we have a greater ally on our side. Tenowk?"

Tenowk looked at him with confusion in his eyes at first, then understanding. "The power...it's surging through me. It's like nothing I've ever felt."

"Give them a command," Lolack said.

For a moment, nothing happened, then there was a loud *clang* sound outside.

"Come," Tenowk said, motioning toward the doors. When they stepped outside, a series of mechs and cyborgs were standing at attention. "Let me try something..." Tenowk lifted a hand to his head, though Valerie imagined it was more to help him focus than anything else.

Suddenly one of the cyborgs stepped forward and attempted a flip. He landed on his tailbone, yelping in pain.

Tenowk shrugged. "Well, I can tell them what to do, but it doesn't mean they can do it."

Lolack turned to Valerie, beaming. "We have our army, and we have our fleet. We have our AI, too."

"In a sense," Tenowk interjected. "I mean, from what I can tell we have to keep it in me, so what am I? Part cyborg, with this new level of control and awareness? I can feel the cyborgs, and even the ship. It's like I can sense things, and—" He froze, raising his face to watch the sky. "Messages... I can hear them."

"You're an IAI," Lolack said with a grin. "Intelligence on

top of Artificial Intelligence. She's inside you, Aranaught is, but we control her now. Call this the next evolution of AI."

"Well, color me as confused as a pig in a flower garden!" Valerie said. "But if it means we win, I'm all for it."

"Oh, we'll win," Lolack said, patting his old friend on the shoulder and then watching Robin approaching with a curious look on her face. The *Grandeur*'s ramp opened and the others emerged, all looking at the mechs with curiosity.

"The ships are nearby," Tenowk said. "Shall we load them up and return to the fleet?"

Lolack turned to Valerie, awaiting her command.

She smiled, then nodded. "Meanwhile, I'll see if Flynn and Lolack can explain to the others what happened here, then send a message to Kalan to let him know we're on our way. I hope they've fared as well as we have.

CHAPTER TWENTY-FOUR

From that point on, the battle was as exhilarating for Kalan as it had to be frustrating and baffling for the Wandarby troops. He'd sent out a distress call and been picked up by one of the fighters, and now he stood on the top of *Flamebird* as the Pallicons attacked. He was in constant motion: firing his Tralen-14, then ducking for cover. He made sure to show himself occasionally to let the Wandarby know that he, the evil Bandian, was here and ready to be taken down if they were tough enough to do so.

As far as he could tell, the Pallicons still hadn't figured out who those mysterious aircraft in the sky belonged to. The Lavkin fighters focused on defending the strange round ships as they visited one Lavkin ship after another.

When they touched down, it was always the same. The doors would open, apparently no one would get out, the doors would close, and the ship would take off again.

And then all the Pallicons attacking one of the nearby ships would die. Some died from gunshot wounds from unseen weapons. Some were stabbed, though there didn't appear to be anyone standing near them. It was an odd sight: Wandarby warriors reeling from a silent and invisible but relentless attack.

That was how most of the combatants experienced the battle. For Kalan and his Shimmer-enabled translation chip, it was quite different.

He heard the war cries and screams of every Shimmer coming off the ship. He heard their invisible commanders barking orders at them. And he heard them laugh in glee as their enemies fell.

While all that was happening around him Kalan fought on, defending his adopted family's ship. Jilla, Bob, and Wearl stood by his side in the thickest part of the battle, taking on an endless wave of Pallicons.

"Wearl, thank the stars for your relatives showing up," Bob shouted to her as they fought off another wave.

She practically spat her response. "They always have their price, and it's usually not worth paying."

Nearly an hour after the Shimmers arrived, the Pallicon assault began to slow. Their numbers were dwindling, and they no longer had the High Priest goading them onward. In fact, Kalan wasn't sure they even had a leader. Each temple seemed to be acting on its own now, attacking as their priest saw fit.

No one officially called off the attack, but they began to retreat one ship at a time.

As the last of the Wandarby soldiers loaded into their ship and fled the Rewot atmosphere, the Lavkins let out a full-throated cheer.

"I don't believe it," Mej said. "We defeated them. We fought off the whole damn Wandarby cult."

Kalan turned, surprised to hear her voice, and he was equally surprised to find Lien standing beside her. He hadn't known the two of them were there; he had no idea when they'd arrived aboard *Flamebird*. For all he knew, Mej and Lien had been fighting by his side for an hour.

"That we did," Lien agreed when he said that aloud, "but not alone. Those were Shimmers fighting by our side, if I'm not mistaken. I take it we have Wearl to thank for that?"

"No," Jilla said slowly, as if just realizing it herself. She turned to Kalan. "You called them, didn't you?"

"Yes," he admitted.

Jilla's lip quivered as she looked at him angrily. "You idiot."

Mej blinked hard. "Sorry, I'm a little out of the loop here. Catch me up?"

Kalan kept his eyes glued to the Shimmer ship resting on the island as he spoke. "The Shimmer Empire has declared me an enemy because I helped someone escape from SEDE. They took it as an affront to their honor. I knew their fleet was nearby searching for me, so I contacted them after the ceremony where you adopted us into the family."

"I still don't understand," Mej admitted. "If you're their enemy, why would they want to help you?"

"I made them a deal. I told them if they helped us fight off the Pallicons, I'd turn myself over to them after the battle." He turned to Bob and Jilla. "We don't have much time. They're going to be here any moment to haul me back to SEDE."

"No way we're letting that happen," Bob said, a growl in his voice.

"Yes, we are," Kalan insisted. "I gave them my word, and I intend to keep it. Look, I've never had much of a family, but you guys," he turned to Mej and Lien, "all of you, you've been a true family. Thanks for everything you've done for me."

"No," Jilla said, blinking back the tears. "This isn't how it ends for us."

"I'm afraid it does, at least for now. Wait here for Valerie to get back with Admiral Lolack. She'll know what to do."

Bob stepped forward and held out his hand. "I don't like it, but I do understand. You're one of the good ones, Kalan Grayhewn. I'm honored to have worked with you."

Kalan took Bob's hand and shook it in the human style, up and down rather than side to side.

Next Jilla stepped forward and fell into his arms. "Goodbye, Kalan."

He hugged her tightly.

Then he said, "Wearl, I—"

"Shut up," she said. "I don't want to talk to you. I'm so angry I could rip your lungs out through your nose."

"I'd rather you didn't. Look, Wearl—"

Something grabbed his arm before he could continue.

A low voice said, "Kalan Grayhewn, you are under arrest for crimes against the Shimmers, their reputation, and their interests. You have agreed to waive a trial, and you are hereby sentenced to the Swarthian Extended Detention Environment for the rest of your natural life."

Kalan smiled sheepishly to his friends. "Looks like they're calling their chip in already."

Mej put a hand on his shoulder. "Thank you, Kalan. Thank you for saving us."

"Anything for family," he said.

The Shimmers shoved him toward the waiting boat that would take them to the island. He took one last look at his friends before turning and heading toward the ship.

As they walked a Shimmer kept a strong hand on his arm, guiding him and letting him know who was in control. He took a deep breath of the salty sea air, knowing it would be the last free breath he took for a long time, and then he stepped onto the ship.

They led him to a row of seats in the cargo hold, each fitted with metal shackles on the arms and legs, all apparently empty. They shoved him toward one, and he sat down. Cold metal touched his skin as they clicked the shackles into place.

Then he waited.

He had no way of telling how much time had passed in the dim light of the cargo hold, but it felt like hours. He tried to cheer himself with the thought that at least he'd see his mother in SEDE. She'd be disappointed in him—after all, her only wish for him had been that he never go back to that place—but at least they'd be together.

SEDE was the last place in the galaxy he wanted to go, but he didn't regret what he'd done. He'd upheld the ancient alliance between the Lavkins and the Bandians, he'd protected his new family, and he'd helped his friends survive. If a trip to SEDE was the price for all that, he was willing to pay it.

Suddenly he heard scuffling and voices raised in anger. A familiar voice shouted, "If you don't get your hands off me, I'll rip them off and shove them down your throat."

A moment later, someone landed hard in the seat next to him. He heard the shackles click into place.

"Now you sit there and keep quiet, you psycho!" a Shimmer shouted.

Kalan waited until he was sure the guards were gone, then said, "Hello, Wearl."

"I'm still mad at you," she replied quickly, "but that doesn't mean I'd let them take you to SEDE without me."

Kalan smiled. "How'd you convince them to bring you along?"

"It was more difficult than I would have thought. First I told them I was the Shimmer who'd escaped with Sslake, but either they didn't believe me or they didn't care. Then I gave one of them a pretty good beating. After that, they were a lot more receptive to the idea of locking me up."

Kalan chuckled. "The guard was right about you being a psycho, but you're also a good friend."

"A friend, and perhaps more once we're in prison together," she said hopefully. "What's Sslake going to say about them locking up the guy who broke him out?"

Kalan thought about that. "I don't think they'll advertise it to him. And if he asks, they'll deny it. Unless he wants to come search SEDE, it would be hard for him to prove they're holding me there."

"So that's it, then? You're going to live the rest of your life in prison?"

He leaned a bit closer to her and spoke softly. "I promised I'd let them take me to SEDE. I never said anything about staying there. How to you feel about helping me plan another prison break?"

Her voice was much cheerier when she answered, "Oh, this is going to be fun."

EPILOGUE

The *Grandeur* was returning to Rewot with Lolack. They were followed by Tenowk, the new IAI—or whatever the hell he was—and their army of mechs and cyborgs. As they drew close to the planet, Valerie's hands clenched and unclenched as she stared at the display.

Not only was it clear a large battle had been fought in their absence, but Kalan had yet to respond to a single message.

"Hailing the *Grandeur*," Mej came through on the display. "Is that really you?"

Valerie stood in front of the screen, smiling despite her worry. "It is, and we've brought you an army. Also..." She stepped aside to reveal Lolack, who stood with Arlay.

"Brother, you're alive!" Mej cried, glancing between him and Arlay.

"I am, and...aren't you going to say anything else here?"

"About the two of you?" Mej grinned. "As long as you're back, I think we can handle Mother and Father. I didn't realize that was her before, though. I mean... Oh, it is the same, right? Arlay?"

Arlay laughed. "Yes, it's the same. Has Lolack been showing up randomly with other blue women?"

"Not a chance," Lolack said, kissing her on the side of the head—not on a tentacle, at least.

"And Kalan?" Valerie asked, turning back to the camera and looking around anxiously. "Is he available? I really must..." As she spoke, Mej's expression grew dark. "What is it?"

"Your friend has been taken into the custody of the Shimmers, I'm afraid." Mej pursed her lips and cast her eyes down. "We would have stopped it if possible, but he insisted on going."

Valerie turned to Robin, who had an equally perplexed look on her face. This was a conundrum—enemy fleets were coming in, but their close friend had been arrested. If he had insisted on going, was it to save others, or did he have some plan in the works?

The real question now was whether to go after him and rescue him while there was still a chance, or stay here and fight.

Valerie would land first to touch base on what had happened and get the full report on the situation, then figure out what to do next. Either way, she was certain it was going to be a grand adventure full of near-death experiences, squashing of injustice, and general badassery.

The perfect job for the Prime Enforcer, she thought with a grin.

Writing this book with PT has probably been the most fun in the series, because we didn't hold anything back. What we see here is a lot of closure on threads we've been setting up since book one. That, and we have dinos, sand worms/snakes, and massive fleet battles (in a sense). Mechs, A.I., and all of those science fiction elements that keep us coming back for more.

What's next? One more book in this arc! Before the end, Aeronaut sent for all of her potential allies, meaning the final book is going to be exciting. And then there was Kalan's fate. Oh, man, that's going to mean an interesting book four, right?

On top of that, I'm launching my first pure science fiction series at the end of the month that this book is published (February 2018). It's called the Biotech Wars, and what I mean by pure is that it doesn't have actual magical elements—no fantasy. It DOES have genetic engineering of the Bourne Identity type, and has alien tech... but should fall into the science fiction realms. No magic fireballs or any of that.

Thank you so much for sticking with us to this point! We'll keep writing them if you keep reading them!

Thank you for reading *Prime Enforcer*.

People seem to be having a lot of fun reading the Valerie's Elites series, but I assure you we're having even more fun writing it.

Working with Justin on these books has been an experience and a half. He thinks fast, moves fast, and writes fast. And his work ethic is inspiring. He lives on the West Coast, and I live on the East Coast, but somehow he still manages to get a couple thousand words in before I get even get up in the morning—and I'm not a late sleeper.

Prime Enforcer was an especially fun book to write. I'm a big fan of movies like *The Seven Samurai*, *The Magnificent Seven*, and *The Thirteenth Warrior* (our great editor Lynne disagrees with me on this last one, but I stand by it). I love stories of a band of warriors coming together to train and protect a small settlement. Kalan's story in this book is sort of a tribute to those types of tales.

Thanks once again to Justin, Michael, Craig, Lynne,

Steve, the JIT readers, and the whole team at LMBPN Publishing. You folks put the "pro" in prolific.

You're probably thinking to yourself, "What else are you up to, PT?"

I'm glad you asked.

The sequel to *The Savage Earth* is finished, and will be hitting virtual shelves in March. I'm very excited about it. My co-author Jonathan Benecke is a genius at crafting intense, pulse-pounding, fun action scenes, and he's really outdone himself this time, so keep an eye out for that!

And I'm very excited about the fourth Valerie's Elites book. Justin and I have been talking about this one for a while, and it's going to be a thrilling and fun culmination of the storylines that have been building in the first three books.

I can't wait for you to read it. The best is yet to come.

Until then, happy reading!

PT Hylton